# ROUGH MEN

# ROUGH MEN

## ARIC DAVIS

**THOMAS & MERCER**

Text copyright © 2012 Aric Davis
All rights reserved.
Printed in the United States of America.

Published by Thomas & Mercer
P.O. Box 400818
Las Vegas, NV 89140

ISBN-13: 9781612186535
ISBN-10: 161218653X

*Dedicated to the memory of Officer Trevor Slot*

**A**lex pushed the magazine into the Glock, pulled back the slide to verify the still-chambered round of .45 ACP ammunition, and then hit the magazine release again. His hands were made of nervous energy, and messing with the gun was as good a way to burn it off as any. The blunt he'd split with Rob an hour earlier had made him go from relaxed, to paranoid, to lazy, and now he was back to paranoid. He sighed and set the rechecked gun onto the console of the van.

"What the fuck is your problem?" called Chris from the bucket seat behind Alex in the ancient Dodge Caravan. "You acting like you didn't already get your pussy wet, homey."

Alex considered the words, then did his best to ignore them. Killing that so-called snitch bitch earlier in the month had not been on his list of things to do in life. In fact, every moment since then had felt almost dreamlike, as if killing that girl—and she was just a girl, Chris and Mumbo had both confirmed that when they started fucking her a year ago, when she was just fifteen—had been something that had happened to some other Alex. An Alex who didn't regret every second since then, an Alex who wasn't sitting in a van waiting for the manager to leave a Lake Michigan Credit Union, the same manager who had been getting head on a consistent basis from the snitch bitch, the same manager who had wanted to be long gone when they went hot. Also, the same manager who had been paid off so well that he was willing to give up everything to let them run this shit.

Alex looked at the Glock one more time, heard Mumbo's cell phone ring on the kind of ringer that sounded like an old house phone, and then they all watched the manager leave the credit union.

The plan was simple. Alex, Mumbo, and Chris were going to walk into the building while Rob drove around it. The manager had been intentionally getting sloppy about the vault for just over six months, so when the blame game started, he would just look like a shitty employee, not like someone who was in on the action. Alex didn't think it was going to make much of a difference. The dudes that set this whole thing up had made it very clear to him that he could come along for the ride and get paid or crash and burn. Alex figured the guy was fucked no matter the take from the credit union; he didn't see any way that he was going to get to just walk away.

Rob gave him a look that said, *Get on with it*, and Alex stopped worrying about managers. He stuffed the Glock in a loose jacket pocket and got out of the van. He had a black duffel in his left hand and took a moment to pull a stocking cap over his face. Chris and Mumbo were doing the same thing with their own ski masks, but neither of them had bothered to try to disguise their guns.

Mumbo was carrying an AK-47 with a folding stock and a short barrel. Chris had a pistol that he'd said was called "the Judge," a Brazilian shotgun in pistol form, which could fire .45 pistol loads as well as .410 shotshells. Alex followed their lead and took the Glock from his pocket before following Mumbo through the door and into the building.

Their sudden appearance shocked the packed room quiet, and then a little girl began to scream. Mumbo was rushing past him to the center of the room, and Chris vaulted over a teller's desk. "Get the fuck back!" he screamed. "Get away from your fucking desks right now!"

Alex could see three loan officers sitting at desks to his left. One of them had been meeting with a client. This guy, the client, and one of the other loan officers rose and moved away from their desks. The one who wasn't moving, a slick-looking younger guy who looked like he should've been selling cars, had both hands under his desk, and without thinking, Alex raised the Glock and shot him twice in the chest.

The explosions were louder than hell in the small building, and now it felt like everyone was screaming, and Chris was repeating his mantras of "Get the fuck down!" and "Stay the fuck away from your desks!"

Alex leaped over the row of teller desks and joined Chris, who called to Mumbo, "You got this?"

"You know I do," said Mumbo. "Now hurry the fuck up."

Alex followed Chris to the waiting vault. It was open just as it was supposed to be, and on one of the walls was a rack of banded bills—hundreds, fifties, and twenties. Alex fell to his knees and began throwing money into his duffel bag, the duffel becoming heavy with bills almost instantly. The sound of gunfire began pouring in from the main floor of the credit union, and then Mumbo was yelling something undistinguishable.

Realizing that Chris wasn't gathering money with him, Alex looked over his shoulder at him. Chris was pulling some things, papers it looked like, from a safety deposit box with a pair of keys still dangling from its lock. Chris locked eyes with him, then turned back to slam the box closed before tossing it onto the floor and wheeling toward Alex, knocking a shelf of money all over the floor as he did so.

Alex and Chris were scurrying like rats, filling their bags until they were impossibly full and then sprinting from the vault together. Mumbo had turned the credit union to a hellhole in the ninety seconds they'd been gone. Two tellers were dead and so were the remaining loan officers, as well as the customer one of them had been talking to when they'd entered.

"Jesus," said Chris, "the fuck happened?"

Mumbo just grunted, and then they were out of the bank, running to Rob as he pulled the van around, exactly two minutes after they'd entered the building.

They yanked open the doors and piled in, throwing the bags into the backseat.

Alex felt like his heart was going to pound free from his chest. *That was like being in a fucking movie.* Killing the man in the bank hadn't felt like doing the snitch—they both deserved it, but the fucker in the bank had been trying to burn them, maybe even thought he had before he'd gotten shot. Alex set the Glock on his lap and pulled the mask off of his face as the van ripped free from the parking lot.

"What happened in there?" said Rob. "Sounded like I was back in Iraq, shit hitting the fan, am I right?"

"We had to put heat on some motherfuckers," said Mumbo. "They wasn't listening good enough."

"I hope it was worth it," said Rob. "Every fucking cop in the county is going to be on this shit."

"Calm down," said Chris. "What happened was only what had to happen, you knew that going in. Hey, don't forget, you turn up there, after that light."

"Do you want to fucking drive?" Rob said, scowling. "You asked me to drive, now let me drive."

Barely audible sirens could be heard in the distance, and Alex looked over his shoulder. Between Mumbo and Chris, he could see traffic at a standstill by the credit union, but no cops, at least not yet.

Rob turned onto their road, and Alex could see the old barn where they'd stashed the other car and the shit to burn the van. "Hurry up," called Chris. "We need to get the fuck out of this car."

Rob just grunted in response and gravel flew under their wheels as they pulled into the farm's forgotten driveway. The barn doors away from the road were open and waiting, and Rob pulled right in, stopping with a lurch that almost knocked Alex's Glock to the floor.

Alex was second out of the van, after Chris, and Mumbo was handing them the bags from the back. By the time Alex got to the Impala, Rob had already gotten the trunk open, and he threw his bag in. Chris set his in after Alex, and almost as an afterthought, Alex looked at Chris and said, "What was up with that safety deposit box, dude?"

Chris looked over his shoulder at Mumbo, who was still next to the van, then turned back to Alex. He raised the Judge, and Alex didn't even have time to react before thunder from the gun took apart half of his head.

**W**ill Daniels was suffering through a severe case of writer's block. His publisher had recently rejected his new manuscript, not that he faulted them for the decision, but if he wanted to belly up to the queue and keep this full-time writer thing going, he needed a story, and he needed it now.

But he had nothing. Hour upon hour, day upon day—nothing.

That had never happened to him before. Ideas had come from the wellspring of his mind as though they were supposed to be there; he'd never had to ferret one out before. They just, well, they just came to him, and he'd never even bothered to say thank you.

It was almost funny. He'd always had such a cavalier attitude about his ideas and work. "Plumbers don't get plumber's block," he'd said on more than one occasion, but those words left a mocking echo now, to say the very least. The cursor was teasing him, blinking over and over again. He'd tried just about everything to force an idea from his head, and nothing he'd come up with had been worth a damn.

Sure, Will had started stuff, gotten up to a few hundred words on some of them, but reading them later, it was clear that they had obviously been forced out by a man playing at being a writer. It was so damn frustrating! Every idea he had was either too similar to something he'd read recently or just plain old sucked. The worst part was that it wasn't like his publisher had such high expectations for him. All they wanted was a manuscript that would be easy to market and sell. Really, he should have the world by the balls. But Will felt like he'd taken a melon baller to his brain getting his first two books on paper.

Will's first published novel had been a YA book titled *The Fort*. A clean little story engine, it had just popped, whole, into his head: Three boys find an old tree house in the woods, and while they're playing in it one day, they look down and see a man kill a young girl. The boys tell their parents, and a massive search is called, but no body or evidence is recovered, and the boys are accused of lying for attention. Since no one else is trying to solve the crime, or even believes that one was committed, the boys decide to solve it themselves.

*The Fort* had sold only moderately well, but the reviews had been amazing. Will hadn't minded a bit that it had brought him only a pittance. He had created something of worth that both his publisher and the critical world at large agreed had merit.

The reception to the second book had been much different. *Broken Bottles* had been written as a supernatural horror novel about a bartender, his friends, and the things that they were losing while they ignored the reality of their collapsing lives. That book had come easily to Will as well, though it had cut closer to the bone. Like his hero, he'd been working as a bartender his entire adult life; the bartender in the book had a caring wife and a fuckup for a son, just like he did; and they were both desperate to escape the bar scene and make life right for their families. The bartender in the book, a man named Trent, had been unable to escape his demons, both real and those created by a mind poisoned by drink. Will had better luck.

*Broken Bottles* earned lukewarm reviews—nothing crazy terrible or crazy good, just sort of "meh." In a perverse reversal of his first book's fate, though, his publisher had sold the hell out of *Broken Bottles*, tepid critical reception be damned. And the second book's sales lit up the demand for his first one. Fewer than six months after *Bottles* had debuted on shelves and Kindles,

Will really did escape from his bartending job, a fate Trent was not to share in the novel.

Retiring from the bar, and the bar scene, had likely saved his life and had certainly saved his marriage. Alison was a fighter. She'd been there for him while he'd worked at all hours and drank like a fish, but she'd turned colder on both counts the older he got, and colder still after his fortieth birthday. The success of *Bottles* had been a miracle for them, or at least as close to one as Will would ever allow himself to believe in.

But now, if he didn't get his shit together, he was going to need another miracle, and the prospects of that were dim as hell.

Going back to the bar after leaving with such fanfare wasn't an option his brain could quite wrap itself around. It wasn't like he wouldn't get the job back; he'd likely be met with open arms. He'd created most of his bad memories there years earlier, back when he still needed cocaine to stay up late and was hitting on everything with a short skirt and a pulse, marriage or no marriage. Alison had never busted him—not exactly, anyway. But his sad, drunken misadventures with other sad drunks had cast a sheen of doubt over their struggling marriage like a caul.

It had never been just about the infidelity, the bottomless bottles of booze, or the work that never seemed to stop. Alex, his son from a long-gone former girlfriend, had been as much of a problem as everything else combined.

Will himself had run with a bad crowd when he was young, had done a lot of drugs and some worse things that he wasn't too proud of. But the arrival of his son, the departure of the boy's mother, and picking just the right night to bow out of an ill-fated smash-and-grab B and E—all occurring within a year of one another—had combined to shake most of the wild from him.

Nothing like that had happened to Alex.

Will had never gotten the right handle on his son. God knew it wasn't Alison's fault, though she blamed herself, despite the fact that he'd been five when they'd gotten married. Alex had just always been off, and the resentment over his missing mother just never seemed to go away, even when it would seem like things were fine for weeks and even months at a time. The boy had gone from skipping school and smoking when he was only eight, to shoplifting and drug use before he'd dropped out of middle school, to finally wind up in the alternative high school a year early. Not that he stayed there, of course. At sixteen, Alex was gone.

Will and Alison heard from him on occasion in the five years after that, but they'd never been able to spare the money he was looking for, and the trips to see him in jail were always awful. Alex was piling up a record that would have made even a young Will pale and forced the older one to the bar—but also, to the keyboard.

Now, sitting before his pitiless cursor, Will felt as stumped as he had raising Alex. When those threads had come loose in his fingers, Alison had picked up the pieces and let him hide from his damaged son in work. Writing had come as a blessing in the years after Alex had mostly disappeared, but now, sitting with no muse, no contact with his son, and a wife almost certainly expecting him to come to bed soon, it was all Will could do not to drink.

He still did partake, of course, and even put on like he could still be the life of the party if he would just let himself cut loose, yet that drinking was tempered, an act for friends that was trying to say that he really could just have a couple and still have fun. Alison had long ago forbade alcohol in the house—a reasonable rule, considering his unreasonable past. He didn't think alcohol would help—not really. But it would be a temporary tarred patch of gravel to soothe the raw road of invention he felt, as though he were carving into his brain.

It had all become a pretty straightforward situation in his mind, and one he was scared to even tell Alison about. In order for him to stay away from booze—or a twelve-step program—he had to write. If he slipped on a brown bag of the good stuff, he was one day closer to working in the bar again, and working there was what had inspired so many benders in the first place. So to make it all work the way he wanted it to, he needed to write, stave off the demon on his own, and not work in the bar ever again. Yet, at the same time, he felt a terribly selfish need to hang onto liquor as well. He wanted more than anything to be the man he never had been, the guy who had a scotch with dinner and could stop right there. He wanted to be himself, a man that the bar wasn't in control of, but for that, he needed a story, and stories can be hard to find when you go looking for one, rather than letting one find you.

Checking the clock on the bottom right of his laptop screen, Will considered the time. 12:30 a.m. Though there was nothing to wake up for tomorrow but the fucking ever-blinking cursor, he'd once again neglected his bed and his wife for far too long. He folded the laptop closed and trudged upstairs, depressed and a little shocked that, once again, he'd gone a day with nothing to show for it and certainly nothing to offer his publisher for the following year.

Will brushed his teeth, spitting into the sink and running wet hands over his face, then made the mistake of looking up. He was somehow still surprised on a daily basis just how old, how haggard and gray, that young man he used to be was getting. It was like looking into a mirror that broadcast the future. He certainly didn't feel different than he had as a kid. More easily tired, maybe, and certainly with less of a temper, but despite his mirror's insistence that he was slowly turning into an old picture of his father, he still felt like Will.

He shut off the water and then the light, flicked off the hallway light behind him as he walked into the bedroom, and slid under the sheets, feeling Alison's warmth and smelling her, two things he could never imagine tiring of.

"Nothing?" she asked the dark. "No luck?"

"No," said Will. "But how did you know, and why aren't you asleep?"

"If you'd been writing, I'd have heard your fingers, at least a little bit, when your fingers really started attacking the keyboard. Or did you forget killing a laptop on the last one?"

He hadn't forgotten. He'd felt like an idiot when the keys had started turning to dead zones under his fingers. Not that the machine hadn't already been on its last legs—dead pixels speckling the screen like dirt, shutting off on its own whenever it felt overworked. He'd taken to writing at the library before shifts, which had only come to light when Alison told him she was leaving if he didn't either come clean about the girl or tell him what the hell was going on. When he'd come home from the bar that night—bombed—a new laptop was sitting on his desk. He'd written until morning, drunk or not, and the chapters smashed into the new keyboard that night had forged a part of *Bottles* that was among those he was most proud of.

Alison switched on the bedside lamp and then turned, leaning toward him on an elbow, her nightie shifting in a way that would have been very enticing if Will had managed to expel even a few words downstairs.

"You know," she said, "I could go back to school. I only need a few more credits, a year tops, and I'd be all set. We've got enough money now to get us there, and it's not like they're not still selling."

"If you want to go back to school, that's fine with me, but don't do it on my account. I'm the one who thought he was a big shot and ready to get out of the fucking bar."

Alison frowned, and Will was sorry he'd mentioned the bar at all. Some things, though in the past, will always show a person's scars off for the world to see, and for Alison, those scars had been left by Will, with the bar as an unwitting accomplice.

"I'm not going back," he assured her. "I'm just saying maybe I left a little early. Maybe my muse needs me to work to generate ideas."

"If that's all your muse needs," smirked Alison, "tell her to get your ass out back and weed my garden."

She smiled at him, the same smile that had made him notice her in the first place, that had made him fall in love with her, and that made him still love her. She wasn't like him: her face was maturing with age, not suffering like his, not turning into the father he'd hated and respected right up until the old man put his hand over his heart, said, "I feel like shit," and died right there at dinner. A quiet joke in the family that could still get some yucks if his brother Isaac and he were drinking—the only time Dad had ever dared swear at the dinner table and it had taken him fucking dying to do it.

"I'm going to get some beauty sleep," said Alison, "and you, my writer man, you get some sleep and find that muse and tell her to give you some words. You're good at this. Beating yourself up is just going to make it worse."

"Yes, ma'am," he said as she turned off the light. "We'll both get those winks we need to look and write good tomorrow."

Nestling back into him, she said, "Well, I'm going to look good tomorrow, either way."

"Fair point," said Will as he closed his eyes, and just like every other night when he'd been positive he'd never sleep, he was out before he knew what had hit him.

**"W***ill***."** Alison was shaking on his arm like she meant to tear it off. Her tone charged with hushed, dead-of-night panic, she said, "Get up, right now! I think someone's trying to break in!"

He was awake then, awake and moving: peeling off the covers, opening the drawer of his nightstand, taking out the loaded Sig Sauer 1911 and SureFire flashlight. Alison was holding a 9mm Sig of her own. She looked terrified but determined. *Is tonight the night that our son and his asshole friends break in?* They'd been worried about it for so long, had been readying themselves for it, though they'd never said as much to each other. What else would the guns have been for?

Will walked out of the bedroom, the Sig pointed at the floor with his finger on the trigger guard and the still-off flashlight balanced in his other hand.

He crept down the stairs. The beating on the door started up again. *A distraction*, thought Will. *Why else would they be knocking?* He'd seen the clock, it was past three in the morning. The knocking continued, and Will moved off the steps, checking left and right of the foyer, dining room, then the parlor, before stepping close to the door.

"I don't know who you are," he called, "but I'm armed, and it would be a good idea for you to leave."

The beating stopped, introducing a silence like a living thing. It seemed to last for minutes, yet was only seconds in length. Finally, the door knocker spoke.

"Sir, I am a detective with the Kent County Sheriff's Department. I would ask that you disarm yourself and open the door. I will not be pleased if you are still holding a weapon when you do so."

*Could it be a trick?* Will pushed the thought aside. If it was, it was a good one. He set his gun and flashlight down on the table next to the door, atop a pile of ignored mail.

"My door is bolted and chained," he called. "I have set down my firearm and will release the bolt, but not the chain. If you don't mind, slip me one of your cards through the gap."

Will undid the bolt, staring at the 1911 on the table, knowing that this probably was a cop and that everything was going to be fine. *Alex got arrested again, maybe graduated to something really bad this time.* Except, that really didn't ring true. Cops don't come around like errand boys to let someone know that their asshole son has been arrested, much less detectives. These thoughts overpowered his fear of an intruder, and feeling quite numb, Will released the chain and opened the door.

The detective standing before him was holding a white business card in his fingers. Startled to have the door swing open so rapidly, the detective's hand went to his hip, the card falling to the ice-spattered stoop. Will could feel eyes probing him for a gun. None of this was going right. Why was this cop here at all?

Convinced Will was unarmed, the detective knelt to retrieve the card. It had a damp corner, but was otherwise immaculate. The detective handed it to him, and Will read it as the detective said his name, Detective Dick Van Endel. He was of just above average height and build, a little paunchy around the midsection, and had a mustache that was more salt than pepper.

"Are you Will Daniels?" said Van Endel, and it was all Will could do to nod, knowing already what was to come, but praying the words wouldn't come from this stranger's mouth.

"Mr. Daniels, I have some terrible news. Your son, Alex Daniels, was found dead three days ago."

"Three days," Will repeated. He gave his head a short, hard shake, trying to process this. "My boy's been dead for three fucking days, and you come to my house in the middle of the goddamn night? Are you insane? Why wasn't I notified immediately?"

"Mr. Daniels, would you mind if I stepped inside? There's a few things you have to know, and I'm sure you're going to have more questions."

"Who is it, Will?" called Alison from the darkness at the top of the stairs, and both men jumped at her voice.

"It's a detective, Ally. Why don't you set down your pistol and come on down here? He has some bad news for us."

Alison was there in an instant, the color drained from her face. "He's dead, isn't he?" she stammered. "Alex is dead? Is our son dead?"

Detective Van Endel nodded grimly. "I'm sorry to say that he is, ma'am. Would you and Mr. Daniels mind if I came in so we could talk about this further? I was just telling your husband—"

"He's been dead for three fucking days," Will spat, unable to hold back the rage in his voice. "Our son has been dead for three days, and this is how they tell us."

Alison's face somehow paled even further; her skin was practically translucent now. In a very small voice, she said, "Why don't you come in, detective? I'll put some coffee on."

Will watched incredulously as this detective, this liar, was allowed into his home. How could Alex have been dead for three days without them knowing? More importantly, how could his son, as troubled as he was, be dead at all? Van Endel passed him, and then Will followed his wife and the detective into their kitchen, his mind full of black thoughts. His only son was dead.

For the first time in a great while, Will had completely forgotten about his writer's block.

* * *

Will made the coffee, despite Alison's suggestion that she would do so. It was a ritual he'd been in charge of from the start of their relationship. This had its genesis in his alcoholism: only he could balance exactly what his stomach could tolerate against how strong he needed the coffee to be in order for him to function. Drinking or not, and these days mostly not, the job of making coffee was still his. Will made the coffee with fingers that seemed to have lost all muscle memory, every action requiring complex thought as he loaded the water and ground beans into the machine.

"Your son, Alex, was found shot to death in an abandoned barn about two miles from the East Beltline," said Van Endel, "on the north end, between Plainfield and Rockford."

"I still don't understand why it took three days for you to tell us what was going on," Will said with conscious effort, containing his rage as he poured a measured scoop of grounds into the cone-shaped coffee filter. "We have rights, and if you think I won't be calling my lawyer in the morning, you're sadly mistaken—"

"Will," said Alison, "make the coffee and let the man speak. There's clearly more to it, right, Detective?"

"Yes, ma'am. I want to warn you, though. What I'm going to tell you will explain why we were unable to contact you, but it's probably going to make this a good deal harder for both of you."

"We can handle it," Will said.

Van Endel nodded, then turned to Alison. "Are you sure you feel the same way, Mrs. Daniels?"

Alison nodded, and Will could see the truth sinking in on her face, now looking nearly jaundiced under the kitchen lighting.

"Your son was found burned beyond recognition in the remains of an abandoned barn, next to a van that had also been burned. The van, and your son, are both considered to have been involved in the robbery and killings that took place at the Lake

Michigan Credit Union branch a few miles from there. You've heard about that robbery?"

Will mouthed assent, and Alison nodded. *Alex was involved in that bloodbath?* The robbery was all the news had been talking about for days, how three armed gunmen had broken that ancient rule of armed robbery, gunning down innocent people who'd been doing what they had been told. "Here's what we know so far: At eleven forty-five a.m. on Tuesday, your son and two other men entered the credit union. One of the men, who I believe to be Alex, shot a loan officer who was attempting to trigger the silent alarm. Alex and one of the other suspects went into the vault—there's video of them stealing a great deal of marked bills—and the third accomplice opened fire with a rifle inside the credit union lobby.

"As you might've heard, four people have been pronounced dead, not counting Alex, with two more in critical condition. None of those people are likely to survive. One of them is a little girl who was shot in the back of the head. She was there with her parents, both of whom are dead now. Even if she does live, she's going to be a vegetable."

Detective Van Endel looked at his hands, which he'd begun clenching and then unclenching as he spoke. Now he opened his fists one last time and laid his palms flat on the glass tabletop.

"The three suspects then left the credit union and got in a van, believed to be the one found burned along with your son, and disappeared. Smoke led us to the fire, which was very far along by the time the firefighters could get to it. Even so, a fragment of your son's driver's license was discovered intact in what little was left of his wallet. We're—"

"So you're not sure," Will said. "That body could've been—"

Van Endel lifted one palm from the tabletop to quiet him. "I'm sorry, sir. And, yes, we'll need your help to obtain your son's dental records. But I don't want to provide you any false hope. We're quite certain the body is your son's. I apologize again for the delay in relaying this information to you. For what it's worth, I've only just come from the lab."

Will's mind spun pointlessly for a while, and then he found himself saying, "Yes. He was always difficult. More than just difficult. But Alex...he would never kill another person. Not without good reason. I know my son. I...I knew him..."

"I only know what I see, sir. I see it over and over, though. I would guess that your son went to jail thinking he was a bad dude and then came out friends with some truly bad dudes. And then maybe these dudes talked him into doing some things you just can't imagine him doing. It's a terrible thing, but it happens. As I said, I've seen it over and over. And then it's likely that he either offended one of his partners or, who knows, questioned the killings. There could be a hundred different reasons for them to have turned on him."

Will tried to imagine Alex pushing back on the killers, facing up to them. It was a stretch. He couldn't imagine his son killing anybody, but he couldn't see him playing such a noble part, either. All the same, he appreciated Van Endel offering up the possibility.

"So what now?" Alison asked. "What do we do now?"

"Well, we're going to have to wait for forensics to finish up with Alex before we can release the body to you. It might not be a bad idea to talk to your church, if you have one, and whatever your family prefers for funeral arrangements."

"What are the chances that the men who killed my son will be caught?" said Will. The edge was back in his voice; he tried to temper it as the words came out, but it didn't work.

"It's highly likely that some manner of evidence will make itself known. That could be through Alex's associations behind bars or his friends on the outside. Someone knows what happened to him, and they had to have been pretty tight if they trusted him enough to rob a bank with them. That person is still out there, and I will find him, I truly believe that. Do you have any more questions for me?"

Alison shook her head, and Will muttered a barely audible no.

"If you come up with anything later, please, let me know. Also, if you can think of anyone who would have wanted to hurt your son, or who he may have associated with in the past, let me know." Detective Van Endel stood. "I'm truly sorry about your loss."

Will stood and shook Van Endel's hand and then led the detective out into the blowing snow.

**W**ill woke just after 6:00, surprised that he'd been able to sleep. Alison gone from their bed was confirmation that none of it had been a dream, that Alex really was dead. He pulled on a pair of warm-up pants, brushed his teeth, and went downstairs.

Alison was waiting for him at the kitchen table, in the seat she'd been in when they'd talked to the detective the night before. She was drinking the coffee that he'd made, then had forgotten to have or share with the detective. She looked at him and said, "I hope you don't blame me for any of this."

"You?" said Will. "Why in the world would I blame you?"

"I'm the one who raised him. I was his mother, whether I birthed him or not. He's my only child, and now he's dead. You put me in charge of one thing—the most important thing—and now he's gone. We could have done more; I should have done more!"

Will sat and moved to grab her hand, but she snatched it away. "Look," he said, "there's no blaming you or anyone else that wasn't there when he died. Alex made some bad choices, and as hard as this is going to be, we don't need to beat each other up over it."

Will didn't say what he thought then, which was that the media wasn't going to need their help to beat up what was left of their family. Alex was going to be a scapegoat for the crimes that had taken place before his death, and nothing was going to change that until his murderers were caught, and even that wouldn't be good enough for those who really knew the victims. Nothing was ever going to be the same, and there was nothing he could do about it.

"I'm going to wait a couple of hours," Will said, "and then I'm going to call my brother and Lou. I need to give Isaac a heads-up about Alex, and I want to talk to Lou about getting our ducks in a row, legally speaking. Before I do any of that, though, we need to talk about what we want to happen."

"You mean with Alex?"

"Yes."

She sipped from her coffee. Will could feel her hollow eyes looking through him. Alex had been her son more than his, even though she shared no blood with the boy. It was at that precise instant that he realized just how awful a father he'd been and that there never was going to be a moment when Alex turned his life around or when the two of them could make things right, to correct the sins of the father and of the son.

"You mean like, what are we going to do with him, once the cops release the body? Because we had a plan. Do you want to change it? He's still your son! He's still my son, and nothing he did changes what we wanted for him, dead or alive."

"I guess it seems weird," stammered Will. "With what happened to him, I feel odd going through with a cremation. It seems morbid, almost cruel, and even if we do, are we still going to want—"

"We have had a will written since you turned thirty," she said, her voice slowly rising, "and nowhere in it does it say that if our son does something too awful, we don't want his ashes spread where ours are going to be spread. He is my fucking son, and you are not going to let something he probably did high out of his mind affect where he ends up now. He was a troubled boy, and he died a troubled death. That doesn't mean that he couldn't be sweet and that we didn't love him." Alison's speech sputtered off and turned to tears.

Unsure if he should try to comfort her, Will instead did nothing, just sat at his kitchen table feeling like the worst person in the world, a man who had failed his child.

Her anger shocked him. He knew it had come from a deep well of dislike that she suppressed, dislike for him and his many failings as a man, husband, and father.

He took her hand. She didn't snatch it away this time, not yet. "You're right," he said, "completely right. When I talk to Lou, I'll have him do what needs to be done to get Isaac to the funeral home. I've never dealt with anything like this before, not as the person who has to help make things happen, and I'm terrified I'll get it wrong somehow."

Alison squeezed his hand and almost smiled at him. "We're going to do fine. There are worse things ahead than just planning a funeral. This all feels like a dream; pretty soon it won't feel like that at all."

Will wanted to say something, to correct her, to let her know that everything really would be all right. Instead, he stood and poured himself a cup of coffee, feeling like he was watching himself in a dream.

\* \* \*

Will left Alison in the kitchen, punching his older brother's number into his cell phone as he went. As it began to ring, he took a seat on the couch and tried to settle on the last time they had talked and figured it had to have happened around Christmas, though he had no memory of it. *How sad is that? I'm calling my brother to ask him for help, and I can't even remember the last time we talked.*

Isaac answered on the third ring, and the call had obviously awakened him. In any other circumstance, Will would have felt terrible, but of course, this was different.

"Will?"

"Yeah, man, sorry for calling so early."

"Is everything all right?"

"No, not at all."

"When did she leave?"

"What? No, man, Ally is still here. It's Alex. He's dead."

Will could practically hear his older brother waking up, as if he'd dumped a bucket of ice water over him.

"What? Alex? How?"

"He was shot to death. We found out last night. Did you hear about the bank robbery here?"

"Yes, of course," said Isaac, his voice broken. "I only live an hour away; we still get the news." Then, slowly, Isaac understood. "Was he a part of that?"

*This is it, the lowest point of my life, when I tell people that my son was in a bank when it got robbed, that he killed an innocent man.*

"He was. I'm sure there will be more information on the news soon, but you can hear it from me first. Something got crooked with him and his dickbag buddies. One of them shot Alex, and then they set him on fire." Will choked for a second, took a deep breath, and continued. "Cops found the body three days ago, within an hour or so after the robbery scene was secured, I would reckon. They're going to pull dental records to confirm it for sure, but yeah, they're sure it's him. He's in bad shape; I haven't seen him, and think it might be best for my own sanity if I don't."

"When do you need me to come up there?"

"I don't need you to, not exactly. Alison and I are going to give him the same sendoff we'd always planned—pour his ashes by the Mackinac Bridge. Same thing we want for our own when the time comes. I'd love if you were up north for that. I'm only calling so that you can know that your little brother is still fucking things up."

Isaac sighed. "You can blame yourself all you want, Will, if that's what you're in the mood for. You and I both know that I love that boy—loved that boy—as much as anyone. But if you and I were bad seeds—and we were—that kid was a bad apple tree, dropping rotten apples all over the place."

Isaac stopped himself, as though he could feel Will's rage rising through the phone. *Why I am I even mad? We both know it's the truth.*

Isaac broke the silence. "I know you're going to blame yourself, and so is Ally, but she was a good mother to him, and you weren't enough of a fuckup to undo all the good she was doing, at least not on your own. That kid was bad stock, no offense, and that led to him getting killed." Another sigh. "You getting mad at me yet?"

"No." Will grinned, in spite of himself. "He was a fuckup. And you're right, so were we. And Mom and Dad were no carnival ride themselves. But we made it out OK. You've done great for years, and I've got my writing thing going now. Why couldn't Alex come around?"

"You're forgetting or lying to yourself," said Isaac, his voice momentarily taking on the agitating static that cell phone users were so used to, then returning to normal. "Took you almost going to jail, maybe even prison, and then going on a bender that only ended when someone gave you a shoulder to cry on and said you could tell stories. Alex never got enough of an eye-opener to make him knock it off. I did, so did you."

"You? What the fuck ever happened to you?"

"The same guys you were running with had older brothers, and if you recall, I quit when I got deep enough in shit. When I discovered that I'd been involved in ripping off a store run by actual tough guys, I decided I'd had enough."

"Why didn't you ever tell me?"

"Will, I've been telling you that story my whole life, you just never felt like listening until right now. I'll be up this afternoon. I'd ask you to have Ally make me a bed, but I think I'll let her mourn and let you do the busywork."

"Thanks, bro," said Will. "I think I'll feel better seeing you in person. I can't feel any worse."

"The next few days, Will, every second is going to be worse."

\* \* \*

Back in the kitchen, Will set his phone on the table and sipped at his coffee. In his dreams, the coffee was a whiskey, his son was alive, he still smoked cigarettes, and his wife didn't look like she might be finally learning how to hate him.

"Isaac coming up?" asked Alison. "It would be nice to see him. Shit, any distraction would be welcome."

"Yep, sounds that way. Might crash on the sofa for a couple days." Pain, again. Alex's room could finally be a guest room. Throw what was left of his stuff out, and there would be a spare space for anyone who needed one. The way things were headed, he himself might need that room. Will felt insane, both desperate for a drink and scared of what might happen were he to have one.

"I'm going to call Lou," he said. "He's either in the office by now or not coming in at all."

Lou answered on the first ring, putting on a feminine voice, and not doing a terrible job of it. "Lou Schultz and Associates."

"Lou, this is Will Daniels."

"One moment please," said the phone, and Will roared back, "Goddamn it, Lou! I know you fired Jen months ago. This is Will Daniels. Can we speak straight? I need to set up a time to see you today."

Nothing but hold music. He hadn't started yelling quickly enough. Or else he had, and his beyond-shady lawyer hadn't liked the sound of it. This was how Lou had always been, all flash, but he'd been even worse since his last divorce. Will sat listening to the Boss doing "Dancing in the Dark" while he waited for his stupid lawyer to stop playing games. Roughly two minutes later, long enough for Will to have to stop himself, twice, from singing along with Springsteen, Lou was on the line.

"This is Lou Schultz, of Lou Schultz and Associates," said Lou in a syrupy sweet voice, the one he'd used years earlier taping the ad that still aired on late-night cable, luring in idiotic drunk drivers and low-level drug offenders. "What can I help you with today, friend?"

"Goddamn it, Lou, knock it off; this is Will Daniels."

"Oh, good to hear from you, buddy." The forced accent had fallen away. "Glad to hear from you. How are things?"

"Not good. My son, Alex, is dead." Will took a deep breath. "Hang on, don't talk yet. There's more to it. The cops are pretty sure he was involved in that credit union shoot-up and that something went wrong later between him and his partners."

"Damn, Will. I'm really sorry to hear that. This is the part where I would usually ask what you want me to do, but how about you just tell me what you're thinking, and I'll offer advice when you're done?"

Will noticed that he was unconsciously drumming his fingers on the table and forced himself to stop.

"The cops are holding Alex's body until their forensic team is done with him. I want you to make sure my son's body makes it to the crematorium. And that's another issue. Alison and I have known for a long time what we wanted done with our bodies, but we never picked a place to do it. Assuming you know of someone you trust, I'd be happy with your advice on that. I think that's everything."

"Well, that's a good start. Do you want me to lean on the cops, see if we can get Alex released any faster?"

"No. He's dead, and I'd rather he was able to help them find out who killed him."

"That's the sensible thing," said Lou. "I thought it was worth asking, though. Makes some people sick, the idea of autopsies and such. All right, well, it does so happen I know a guy who works in the business of cremation, and he does a serious job of it, not one of those assholes you see on the news, you know, triple-stacking bodies and then handing out bags of ash of whomever." A patch of dead air. "Shit, Will. I'm sorry. I shouldn't be talking like that.

"Anyways, I assume the press doesn't know yet, because if they did know, they'd be crawling up your ass by now. First thing you do when we hang up is to change your mailbox messages on your phones and say something like, 'To speak with Will or Alison Daniels, please contact them through their attorney Lou Schultz,' and then tack on my phone number. I'll drop by in a couple hours with a sign that says the same thing that I'll put up in your yard.

"I'm not going to lie, at some point, you're going to have to release some sort of statement, but using me as a buffer will add some time. The next thing you need to do is be ready. I mean, thank god you're not some household name, but people are going to be saying nasty things about you on the web; you might even get a nasty phone call or two. Your son and his friends hurt a lot of people, and no one knows why. It sounds like you're not planning a funeral, but that doesn't mean that you won't have to deal with some serious assholes. That all sound good so far?"

"Yeah. Thanks, Lou. I won't say you made me feel better, but it's nice knowing you have a plan for this sort of thing."

"Will, I hate to be flip in such a sad time, but I've got a plan for just about everything. One last thing, stay away from the news, stay away from the Internet. Don't worry, I'll be in touch, and you can call me if somebody tries to put your nuts in a vice."

* * *

Lou was good to his word; in fact, he was still in the yard installing the sign when the first news van rolled up, this one from Fox 17. Watching Lou and the falling snow through a barely cracked window blind, Will considered going outside, after all. Fox had given him coverage for both books, and he recognized the reporter.

"That's Michelle DePalma," Alison said, now standing next to Will and peeking out. "She looks a little older in person."

"I told you that," Will said, watching Lou shake the reporter's hand. The van drove away just a few minutes after arriving, and Lou went back to his sign. "She's really nice, though."

"She was. She might not be so nice now. I bet a lot of people that we thought were nice are going to treat us differently. The paper and television are going to make Alex into a monster, especially if the other people aren't caught."

Alison closed her eyes for a moment, like she was bearing down against a sharp pain. When she opened them, they were burning into him. "God," she said, "I just realized how bad I want them to get caught. And not just for Alex, either. They did something really horrible, and not only to our family or Alex. All those people who died at that bank. All their families."

Again, she shut her eyes against the hurt in her. When she opened them this time, they were huge and wet. They broke his heart. "They got Alex into a situation where he was doing things that he never would have done," she said, almost whispering now, "and then they killed him."

"It's awful," Will agreed, aware for the first time of the rage building in him. Anger was an emotion he'd gotten skilled at suppressing—booze worked well, writing even better—but now he was angry like he'd been through most of the latter, bitter years of his youth. It had a taste, like iron in his mouth. *What if they don't catch them, and I spend the rest of my life wondering who was with my boy when he died, wondering why they killed him, wondering if he knew he was going to die?* Will's mind wandered to the Sig 1911, and he knew in his heart that, given the chance, he could and would kill the person who had done this to Alex.

Lou waved at them, got into his Cadillac SUV, and drove away. When the truck for News 8 showed up, Will let the blinds fall closed and left the room. Alison followed him.

"When will Isaac be here?" she asked his back.

"As soon as he's able, from the sound of things."

"Good," she said, grabbing Will, spinning him around and wrapping her arms around him. "I'm scared, Will. You keep getting this look on your face, and it's not a good look. I don't know what you're thinking, but when I said I wanted those bastards caught, I meant by the law." She tightened her grip on him and said into his chest, "You need to remember that you're a bartender turned writer. You haven't been in a fistfight in years, you're going to see fifty before you see forty again, and the law is going to handle these guys when they find them. No matter what happens, you need to accept it, even if it's not enough to satisfy either one of us."

Will nodded but knew he was lying when he did. He had a hard streak in him. Those things don't go away; they lay dormant until they're needed. Like a housewife able to lift a car off of a trapped child, Will knew in his heart that if he had half a chance, he would kill the men who had hurt his son.

**W**ill offered to help Isaac carry his stuff in, but his brother had only brought one bag and insisted that Will stay in the house. Once he was settled into Will's office as a temporary bedroom, Isaac assembled with Will and Allison at the kitchen table. Will laid out what Lou had told him, and Isaac agreed with all of it.

"Well, these are about the worst possible circumstances," said Isaac, "but it is nice to see you both. It's been too long."

"We've all been busy," Will said. "That's just how it is when you get old."

"And we've all accepted that's how things are supposed to be," said Alison, "that's the real problem." She took a napkin from a caddie at the center of the table, wiping both eyes and then blowing her nose into it. "I'm glad you were able to come be with us, Isaac. It means a lot. How's Daisy?"

"Daisy's good. She sends her love. She wanted to come, but I told her this wasn't the trip she needed to make. Besides, she has classes all week, and she only gets so much time off. I, however, wouldn't have missed this for anything. Have either of you two eaten since you found out what happened?" Will and Alison shook their heads, and Isaac stood up. "Well, no one ever accused me of being Tom Colicchio, but I imagine I can whip up some food for us. And I don't want to hear any crap about not being hungry; of course you're not hungry, but that doesn't mean you're not going to eat."

Isaac set to banging around in their cupboards, and neither Will nor Alison stood to help. Alison took his hand and squeezed it, but Will felt nothing from the gesture, no warmth, just the rage building in his stomach, and he knew that, eventually, he was going to need to release it on something.

* * *

The doorbell rang constantly despite Lou's sign, but none of them answered it, nor did they check to see who was standing on the stoop. Both Will and Alison's phones rang constantly as well, and after the second reporter called, Isaac switched Will's inbox message to what Lou had suggested.

The two brothers talked little to each other, the old frigidity coming back without effort. Alison seemed not to notice, but Will knew that she could see the divide growing slowly between them. Try as he might, Will knew that Isaac held him at least partially responsible for what had happened to Alex, and knowing that his older brother was right, and polite enough not to mention it, made Will resent him even more, whether it was fair or not.

They slept a fitful sleep, Will with unspeakable and thankfully unremembered nightmares, Alison tossing and turning at his side.

**T**he second day went the same as the first. Alison was quiet, the two brothers' interactions with each other forced. Lou called twice, once to see how they were doing, the next to schedule a meeting for the following afternoon to prepare a press release.

Late in the morning, Will's cell phone rang for what felt like the thousandth time. This time, the screen said Kent County Sheriff's Department. Will answered immediately.

"This is Will Daniels."

"Mr. Daniels, this is Detective Van Endel."

"Do you have information on my son?"

Isaac and Alison had gone dead silent; a pin dropping would have been an explosion in the kitchen.

"Is your wife with you? I'm comfortable with being on speaker if you want her to be able to hear this right from me."

"She is, so is my brother, but this fine."

"All right. Mr. Daniels, this is going to sound like bad news. It's not—at least not all bad—but it's probably not what you were hoping to hear. First off, your son's remains are going to continue to be analyzed by the medical examiner for at least three more days."

"I was hoping to hear you'd caught them. Anything else is all the same to me."

"Your son was shot with a revolver made by the Brazilian firearm manufacturer Taurus; it's a gun called 'the Judge,' and it's basically a shotgun in pistol form."

"How is that legal? I thought shotguns had to be a certain size."

"This Judge pistol rides a legal tightrope, because it has a slightly rifled barrel and can fire pistol rounds along with shotgun shells. It's perfectly legal. Now, here's where the problem starts. Your son was killed by a four-ten shotgun self-defense load. Turns out, even if the Judge had fired a bullet, it wouldn't have carried identifiable rifling marks, but the point's completely moot with a shotgun round. Pellets are pellets."

"So it would be impossible to tell exactly which pistol was used to shoot my son."

"Yes, precisely," said Van Endel. "And of course, that's not the news you were hoping to get. That said, there's only been two other felonies committed with a Judge revolver in the state of Michigan in the last twelve months. One of them was a father who shot his daughter's boyfriend in the stomach and groin with birdshot; the other is a still-unsolved murder that took place about three weeks ago. A sixteen-year-old alleged prostitute named Cassidy Reynolds was shot in the back of the head with a Judge. Just as interesting, her body was burned, with gasoline used as an accelerant, like it was with Alex. And the body was found in Kent County."

Will sucked in air through his teeth, his heart pounding in his chest and his mind racing. "So you think that whoever killed that girl was involved with Alex's death?"

Van Endel snorted. "Hell of a coincidence that the only two unsolved crimes involving one of those pistols took place in the same county, and both on the north end. The problem is that, even if we caught the guy who killed them with the pistol, the gun is basically unlinkable to the crimes. What that means for your son, the girl, and our still-unidentified suspect is that he is going to have to trip up massively in some other way to get caught.

"The plus side, men who rob banks aren't known for good decision making after the fact. First of all, nearly all of the money they stole was marked. If so much as one of those bills turns up again, we'll be able to trace exactly where it was spent, and likely by whom. Secondly, these guys—as messed up as it may sound—are going to be proud of what they did. They're not going to be able to keep it to themselves. Bragging to women, that sort of thing. Luckily for us, that sort of bragging makes the wrong kind of impression on most people, especially women. Third, they might try and pull off something like this again. And maybe they'll make some mistake doing it."

"But you weren't able to find any mistakes they made this time."

"Not yet," sighed Van Endel. "I'm sorry I don't have better news for you, but I figure honesty is the best policy at this point. Speaking of which, is there anything you wanted to tell me about your own history? I know you're a bit removed from that scene, but I have to ask."

Will felt himself redden, shocked to have this soft accusation placed at his feet by the detective, but both the surprise and anger faded quickly. He stood from the table and left the dining room, covering the bottom of the phone with his right hand and ignoring the reactions of his wife and brother.

"Detective Van Endel, there is nothing in my past, even the most checkered parts of it, that attaches me to this robbery in any way. The only guilt I have is that I raised a son who could do something so monstrous."

"I don't mean to offend, Mr. Daniels. You do have to see no small coincidence in your son being involved in this type of activity and your past affiliation with a group pretty well known for similar extracurricular exploits."

Will sighed. "Long time ago. Another world. One that Alex has never had any contact with."

"Maybe so, Mr. Daniels. All I ask is that you think about your past and whether or not anything there could tie into more current events. I'll be in touch, Mr. Daniels. Think about what I said."

The line went dead, and when Will turned, he saw Alison and Isaac standing behind him in the hallway. He felt himself flush, as though they'd caught him at something shameful. Van Endel's digging into his past for some connection made him feel guilty in some perverse way, and he knew that was exactly what Van Endel had intended to happen. If Will were involved, such an accusation would have rattled him to his core, and Van Endel would've sensed it. Instead, it just made Will hate his past even more.

* * *

Will quickly relayed everything that Van Endel had said. His wife and brother had managed to distill most of the conversation from his end of the phone, but he filled them in on the details. There were no other suspects. There were no leads at this time. There was little to hope for. He left out the odd semi accusation that had been lobbed his way, though he could tell by the way Isaac was looking at him that, at the very least, his brother suspected why he had left the room, and Will would have been surprised if his wife didn't suspect the same thing.

"So what now?" Alison asked. "We just wait for the media to leave us alone?"

Will stared at the smoked-glass tabletop. He was bone tired and had never felt so useless—which was saying something, considering the behavior he'd engaged in before getting his head straight.

Isaac spoke up. "One of you mentioned your lawyer wanting to get together to release a statement to the press. Why don't we get hold of him and get that sorted out?"

Will plucked his cell from the table and took it with him down the hall to the entryway. He eased apart two slats in the blinds over the window next to the door and could see at least two news trucks parked in front of the house. *What do they want from us? My son is dead. What could I say that wouldn't be horrible to hear?*

Clicking his phone on, Will called Lou. No shenanigans this time—Lou answered as himself on the first ring.

"Lou, it's Will. I spoke with the police, and Alison and I are ready to stop sitting on our hands and work on the press release that you mentioned."

"Well, I'd hate to even imagine what my colleagues would say about a lawyer who'd make two house calls in the same week—and without raising his rates, no less—but what am I going to do with a pair of shut-ins for clients? You still drawing a crowd outside, I imagine?"

"We should've put in bleachers."

"I'll be over shortly, and you can save the unsatisfying conversation you had with the police for when I get there."

Lou hung up on his end before Will could say anything, and he returned to the kitchen, the one room in the house that had retained any semblance of normalcy.

"Lou's on his way."

\* \* \*

It took Lou a long time to get to them. When he finally did knock at the door, Will, Alison, and Isaac all stood at the same time. Isaac waved them away. "Don't even think about it," he said, and walked to the door.

Will followed most of the way down the hall and watched as his older brother opened the door. In the short window before Lou walked in but the door was open, Will could see cameras pointing at and into his house. Then the door was shut, and Lou and Isaac followed Will back into the kitchen.

It turned out that Lou had arrived only about a half hour after Will had hung up the phone, but it had taken him the better part of another hour to make his way into the house. "Feeding the beast," Lou said, then looked them over. "Will, Alison, how are we holding up?"

"Good," said Alison.

Will just nodded.

"I noticed some family resemblance on your doorman. You are Will's...older brother?"

"Yes. Isaac. Nice to meet you."

The two men shook hands and then sat at the table, Lou across from Will, Isaac across from Alison.

"I'm glad you were able to come visit for a little while, Isaac. These two people are going to need some help, you can be sure of that.

"First things first, I want you guys to get me up to speed on where the cops are at with this whole thing. I'm not at a point where I feel like I need all of your contact with them to be face-to-face with me sitting next to you, or even with me listening in as counsel on phone calls, but we might get there. So where are we at with the law? Do they have any leads?"

Will told most of the story, but Alison and Isaac filled in the gaps, even mentioning things that Will hadn't told them, at least not through words.

"I could tell by watching Will that the detective was prodding him, trying to get some kind of emotional response out of him," said Alison. "I don't see how he would think we were involved. And if he even suspects that, then it must mean that the cops are already desperate."

"Cops are always desperate," said Lou. "That's how people get fucking railroaded all the time. A cop doesn't need to catch the right guy for the crime; he needs to catch a guy that a jury will think is the right guy for the crime. Sometimes that means they catch the bad guys; sometimes it means some poor asshole is up to his knees in bullshit. I had a case a few years ago where a guy I wound up working with had been held for six months on a hundred-thousand-dollar bond for possession of heroin. Now, this poor guy had maintained since day one that the 'heroin' that he had was just a bag of vitamins that had melted together while he ran in the rain. 'Bullshit,' said the cops. 'We tested it. Heroin.'

"Except, guess what? They hadn't, and my client was telling the truth. You will never believe the hurdles I had to jump just to get that judge to finally test the fucking dope. That put some egg on some people's faces, let me tell you. Here's the thing, though. By then, the guy had lost his wife over it, had terrible custody issues, the whole nine yards. I begged that poor asshole to sue the hell out of them, but he wouldn't. Settled out of court for like fifty thousand dollars. Pennies for what he could have had. Pennies for what he deserved."

Lou's story had only made the three of them feel worse, and he must have seen it on their faces. "But seriously, guys? Things like that are few and far between." He clapped his hands. "Let's get to it, then.

"What we need to do now is figure out what exactly you want to say to the press, plus the community at large, and then get it to them. We either establish that you're victims in this— and you are, you've lost your son, for God's sake—or you risk coming off as complicit in what happened. I don't think it does anyone any good to keep on waiting, you or them. What do you want to say?"

"I'm not sure," said Alison. "I guess I would want people to know that, as his mother, this affects me very deeply. And even though I'm as horrified as everyone else by what Alex did, and certainly ashamed, I'm still mourning my son."

"Absolutely. There are a few factors in play here, though, guys. What you say, how it's perceived by the media, and then how that spin is taken by the public. Now, we need to word this in a way that elicits sympathy without coming anywhere close to outright asking for it.

"And then there's the fact that you, Will, are in the public eye a little bit. That's another potential complication. It's extremely important that we handle it right."

Will gave his head a shake as if to jar it into service. "What the hell are you talking about?"

Leo opened palms on the table. "The novels you've written, Will. No one would ever connect them to anything insidious under normal circumstances, but people get killed in both of them—in the second one, quite a number of them, if I recall correctly."

"You are fucking kidding me. Those are *stories.*"

"I'm not saying that it would be fair for you to be judged over a work of fiction, but it's reality. People, and lots of them, are going to be judging your actions as parents, and you need to accept that. No matter how well we spin this, and no matter how well the media behaves, there are still going to be people out there that regard you as, at best, bad parents."

The kitchen went quiet. Outside, an engine rumbled—one of the TV trucks, maybe, shifting its position—then went silent.

A black emptiness yawned open in Will. Like opening a tap, he let the rage fill it. "Well, at worst, what will they think?" he snapped. "We weren't the best parents—me especially—but we did the best we could with Alex." *No, you didn't.* And just like that, the rage drained out of him again.

"That," said Lou, "is the exact opposite of the attitude you need to have. Think contrite. I'm going to put something together, and then we'll all sit here and go over it, and maybe I'll let you make some suggestions, as long as they're polite and you don't make me feel too bad about needing to edit my work. Which reminds me, have you talked to your publisher yet, Will?"

"Shit."

\* \* \*

*Hi Jack,*

*I feel it's necessary to give you an update on the goings-on here in Grand Rapids. I'm not sure how much of this has already reached you. I'm guessing it hasn't yet—I haven't missed any emails from you, and I know you would have at the very least done that—but it will soon, and I wanted to have the chance to tell you myself.*

*Earlier this week my son was involved in a bank robbery, and several people were killed. Alison and I found out a few days after the fact that Alex was involved, when his body was discovered. Everything has been sort of a whirlwind since then. I'm not sure I even would have remembered to give you a heads-up if my lawyer hadn't mentioned that I ought to.*

*As I think you know, my son and I were not very close, but this has still been devastating, as I'm sure you can imagine. The worst part, even worse than Alex's death, is that he could do something like this at all.*

*My family is going to issue a press release later this afternoon. If you could direct any contact that comes your way to my lawyer—I'll add his contact info below—that would be great. If there are other issues involving us continuing to work together after this, I totally understand, and please don't feel that you guys are doing anything wrong if that's the route you have to take. If you have any questions, I will answer them as I am best able.*

*Thanks,*
*Will*

Will stared at the hastily drafted, then painstakingly corrected e-mail before moving the mouse to SEND and clicking the message off to Seattle.

The message was as nice and plain as he was able to make it, and Jack was a great friend who had gone to bat for him on more than one occasion, but Will was still worried about what his and his company's reaction might be. He stared for a while at the cheap wood paneling on the walls, and then his eyes fell to Isaac's stuff piled on the old sofa he kept in the office, and it all looped around to him again. He wasn't going to wake up from this awful dream.

His cell phone ringing broke his trance. Expecting to see another unknown number, Will was startled to see a 206 area code. *Seattle.*

"Hello?"

"Will. Jesus, buddy. You know there are some times when you just pick up a fucking phone and call, right?"

"Thanks, Jack."

"Are you doing OK? How's Alison?"

"I'm OK. She's doing OK, I think. It's been hard to tell. She keeps blaming herself for everything. That's hard to watch."

"That's understandable, I guess. Of course, it's not either of your faults, but it's natural to feel that way. Do you have a time for the funeral set?"

"I don't think we're going to have one. My lawyer thinks I'm in for a shitstorm either way. Not that it really matters much—we had planned for cremation already, anyways. Got a jump on that, at least. That's a good thing, right? Bastards that shot him in the head, they burned his body—"

"Will, you do not sound like you're doing OK. Sit down, on the floor if you have to."

"All right."

"Are you sitting? I'm serious about this. If I hear the phone drop, I'm hanging up and calling nine-one-one. Are you at home?"

"Jack, relax. I'm sitting at my desk. I was letting my emotions get the better of me. I'm fine now."

"Maybe you should try grabbing a drink. But not alone. You've got enough friends, go grab a beer, but don't sit alone with your thoughts."

"No, I haven't been drinking. I think that's for the best."

"Most of the time, I'd agree. This is a little different."

"I'll run it by Alison."

"Is there anything I can do? If there was a funeral, I know we would send flowers. I can fly in, but I'm guessing you want to be with your family."

"I appreciate that, Jack, but, yeah, we're kind of hunkered down. There's nothing you can do. No need for the flowers, either. It's going to be a very small get-together, and I think I'm going to discourage that sort of thing as much as possible."

"Got it. Will, I'd like to respect your privacy, but part of me thinks folks around here should know, especially Terri. She and I are the two people most likely for the media to contact."

"It's fine if you tell the office. I don't want everyone to think I'm some murderer-raising freak, but…"

Dead air for a beat.

Then, "Christ, Will. No one who knows you is going to think that. And we all know you pretty well, even the people here that only know you through your books."

"Thanks, Jack. I really appreciate that. I did have one more question, though. I mentioned it near the end of the e-mail, and—"

"No, no, no, Will. For God's sake, we're not going to drop you for something like this, something that's not your fault. Don't even think about that."

"Thanks, Jack. It's good to hear the words."

"Absolutely. We might need to delay the next book a little bit, is all. It won't do you any good to have this be the only thing people think of when you're mentioned as an author."

"Thanks. I know it should be the least of my worries, but I have been thinking about that a lot."

"Well, I think that's one thing you don't need to think about, beyond what I've said. I'll talk to Terri, maybe even to Bruce, the VP, to be sure we even need to have a delay on your next book."

"To be honest, Jack, a delay isn't a bad idea either way. After the last manuscript was a no go, I've been bone dry in the idea department. I feel like I put everything that I had into it."

"So you wrote a book, and it didn't happen. Big deal. All that really matters is the next one, and then the one after that. I'm not going to give you a pep talk, because I don't think you need one, but bottom line, writers write, so write."

"Jack, I can't say how much I appreciate this."

"If you need anything—and I'm serious, anything—let me know, and I'll do what I can. I'll talk to Terri later and see what she has to say about everything, and on behalf of everyone here, I'm really sorry about what happened to your son."

"Thanks again. I'll talk to you soon."

Will hung up the phone, shut off the light in the basement, and trudged back upstairs to the kitchen.

\* \* \*

*For Immediate Release:*

*We are deeply sorry for the actions of our son, Alex, and regret his role in the crimes committed at Lake Michigan Credit Union Branch 421 on February 18, 2013. It is our deepest wish that the men who committed these crimes with him be brought to justice, and that their victims can take some solace in their punishment. We do not wish to speak further with the media at this time, and appreciate your respect while our family grieves. Further inquiries can be made through our attorney, Lou Schultz, Esq., of Lou Schultz and Associates.*

*Sincerely,*
*William and Alison Daniels*

The media release that Lou had drawn up was perfect. Lou sent it off from the kitchen table, and the thought that the constant media presence could soon be gone, its appetite sated, was welcome news, indeed.

"Well, that's done," said Lou. "Anything else I can do for you today?"

"I don't think so, Lou," Alison said, and to Will, her voice had a strength that it hadn't before. *We're moving forward*, he thought as she went on. "Is there anything else that we should be careful about?"

"Stay the course," said Lou. "Don't watch TV, avoid the web—aside from e-mail, of course—and keep that thick skin on. You're not out of the woods yet—quite the contrary, in fact. Let me know the second the police are willing to release the body, and I'll get my man on it. Will, any interactions you have with the fuzz that involve more than a yes-or-no question should make you prick your ears up. I highly doubt that they'll try anything, but you never know with a cop. They want a name to put on this, and it doesn't matter who it is as long as the crime sticks to the name."

"Thanks, Lou," said Will, and the two shook hands over the table.

**T**hat night, Will sat up in bed next to Alison. They were both pretending to read the books they'd been working through up until their lives had been thrown into a blender that was set to *Destroy*. Will found himself staring at his wife, and after a few minutes of that, she noticed, turning to him to say, "What is it?"

"It was a really special thing you did for Alex," he said. "You took a risk with me, and you raised that boy basically on your own. I love you for so many reasons, but I think that's the one that stands out above everything else. You took Alex and me and made a little family, despite my best efforts to fuck it up. I'm never going to be able to pay you back for that."

Will could feel his eyes welling with tears, and he shook the sad thoughts of his young son and beautiful Alison from his mind. He'd done everything he could to destroy what they had, and she'd just kept chugging right along, making them work, making the family work, struggling far harder than he had to make his son into a man.

"Will, it's fine," Alison said. "There's nothing wrong with being emotional—probably better to just let all of that stuff out. You know that. How else could you write like you do?

"We just have to keep going. We need to get Alex from the police, give him a proper send-off, and remember the good things in his life. Just because he never saw redemption doesn't mean that we can't find redemption for him.

"You've got your writing, and I'm going to find something for myself, whatever it takes to fill this hole in my chest and replace it with something good. I need it to make his life have purpose, so I can say in twenty years, 'I never would have gotten this good done if my son hadn't had such a stupid death.' Does that make sense?"

"Absolutely," said Will, pulling her to him. He wanted her to find that peace; she deserved it. He wanted it for himself too, but he couldn't even see it from the dark place he was living in. Peace, at least right now, seemed the least likely option for him.

"It's all I've been thinking about," she said to his chest. "It's the only thing that keeps the bad stuff away. Sort of like being little and knowing that as long as I had my stuffed bunny, Doug, that nothing bad was going to happen to me. Just like how Doug kept the monsters away, the good thoughts are doing a number on the bad ones."

She pulled back and smiled at him then, and it was all he could do to stifle a sob of joy that this wonderful woman had seen through his dark side for all these years and was still fighting to make a good life with him. At the same time, though, a truly black thought, urged on by the black pool of rage still boiling in his stomach, took root. For the first time, Will had an idea about justice that didn't involve the police.

He kissed his wife, then asked if she'd mind if he went to talk with Isaac for a bit.

"I think that sounds great," she said. "You guys should take advantage of him being here. Catch up. I don't know what it is with you two. You aren't estranged, exactly, but it's like you go out of your way to avoid contact with each other."

"Yeah. I'm not sure what it is, either. It's all kinked up. It's like being apart so much eats at us, and then being together makes us resent all the time apart, and then we just do it all again."

She blinked at him; then they both laughed. "Well, that *is* messed up," she said. "Whatever it is, you have my blessing, and tell Isaac hello for me."

"Yes, ma'am."

As Will clambered out of bed, she said one last thing. "Will? If he has a bottle, you stay out of it, OK?"

The words nearly broke his heart, and he said yes. *Some demons never get all the way gone, no matter how many stuffed bunnies we line our beds with.*

**W**ill stood at the top of the basement steps. His feet were cold, and he was already regretting not bringing socks. His good slippers were downstairs under his writing desk, so at least the cold-feet issue would be settled in a minute.

"Isaac? You awake?"

"Wide-awake."

"I'm coming down."

Isaac grunted at that, and Will began to make his way down the stairs, his frozen feet feeling stupid on the wooden steps, which were covered only in the middle, and there only with very cheap and thin carpeting.

When Will arrived at the bottom of the steps, he found Isaac sitting at his desk, browsing the web on his computer. And wearing his slippers.

Will settled onto the couch next to Isaac's stuff. If his brother was bothered by the intrusion, he didn't show it; he just kept browsing on Will's computer and was currently looking at the Yahoo sports page.

"I need to talk to you about something," Will said, "and I think it's important that you know that, no matter what you say, I'm going through with this."

Isaac turned wearily from the computer and looked at his brother. "I have a bad feeling about this."

"So do I."

Isaac sighed, leaned back in the chair, and gave the computer one last look. "You know March Madness starts soon."

"I don't watch college sports, except for hockey sometimes."

"I'm not worried about what you watch; there's money to be made on State this year. Spit it out."

"I think we need to do something for Alex."

"You mean like, more than the cops are doing?" Isaac looked at him for a long moment. "I think that's a horrible idea."

"I want to go talk to Jason Wixom."

"Jason Wixom?" Isaac said, then began shaking his head back and forth. "No way, Will. No fucking way. That's beyond just a bad idea; that's fucking suicide."

"He might be able to get us information that the cops can't."

"Yeah, he might. He also might beat the shit out of you, put a bullet in your eye, pull out all your teeth, cut off your hands, and bury you in pits of quicklime out by Dorr."

"He was never that bad."

"You ran with a bad bunch, and he was the worst of the lot. Not to mention your old partner Wixom just might still harbor a little bit of a grudge about you taking that unexplained vacation day and then getting off scot-free while he went to go sit in Jackson for five years. Amazing to me you never heard from him when he got out, to clear up that little question. That's the sort of thing that would make anyone curious, if not a little angry, much less a guy like Jason. Besides, how in the hell would you even go about finding him?"

"I know where he works," Will said. "I heard in the bar he owns a tattoo shop on the west side of town. And as for him not coming after me, by the time he got out I had a five-year-old son, and he'd had enough of being locked up. All that time must have made asking why I stayed home and watched TV instead of going to jail with him seem less important."

"OK, so you can find him, great. But I guarantee he knew you worked in a bar, just like you knew about him tattooing. If he wanted to be buddies, why wouldn't he have come by and bent your ear while you served him a few pints of Founders?"

"I don't really care why he didn't come by or what he thinks about me and why I might've stayed away that day. I'm going to talk to him. I'm asking if you'll come with me, and that's it. As much as I appreciate your advice, that's not what I need right now. Unless you have criminal ties still—and we both know that you don't—Jason is the only person we know with a chance to help us."

"What are you going to tell Ally?"

"That we're going grocery shopping."

"She'll believe that?"

"She knows I don't lie to her anymore."

"So you're going to break that trust by lying again."

"It's not like I have a choice."

T hey took Isaac's car, Will giving directions as they drove through the blowing snow and ice-covered streets. His fingers kept finding the Sig Sauer in its shoulder holster, feeling the gun over and over again to be sure it was there and, once reassured, repeating the action again. He was nervous in an indescribable way, as though his whole life had somehow led to this moment, and it still might end up being meaningless.

Alison had said little about them leaving, other than to help put together a list of groceries they needed. And they did need food. Even eating as little as they had been, three adults were churning through what he and Alison had picked up the week before.

*Before.*

List in hand, discreetly holstered pistol under his jacket, Will had ventured with his brother into the snow and aboard Isaac's Toyota Camry.

"I think we should wait to get groceries," Will said. "If something bad happens, it'd be a waste of money to have gotten them first."

Isaac gave a laugh like a cough. "That's very thrifty thinking. You trying to get me to turn the car around?"

"No. I just think we should go talk to Jason first. You know, just get it over with. We're both just going to be on edge until we do it. I'm a wreck."

"Yeah, I noticed. You need to cool it with that gun shit. If Wixom is like he used to be, he'll have you dead before you unzip your coat to get that thing out."

Will scowled at his brother. "I'm not planning on trying to get the drop on him. This is just insurance. And it's not like we're going to walk in and get frisked. He's running a business, and we're going to go in and ask for a few minutes of his time. He'll either oblige us or tell us to get the fuck out, and if he does the latter, then I'll plead our case. The gun is in case he tries to do something else, which, yeah, with a guy like Jason, is a possibility. I don't want to have to use it, but better to have it and not need it than to need it and not have it."

"Yeah, and better to not get caught with it when you're already dealing with someone who hates you. He sees that gun, he'll know we're not all smiles."

"I'm not leaving it in the car."

"I don't want you to," said Isaac as he pulled the Toyota off the highway. "I'm just being honest with you. If you need to use it, you need to just use it, not think about it."

Isaac parked the car in front of the shop. The building was old but not as decrepit as the rest of the neighborhood, which appeared to be doing a brisk business in liquor sales, massage work done by "American girls," and the sale of cheap—but not chain—fast food.

The tattoo shop was painted blue, and the most recent coat looked like it probably should've been scraped and redone about two years prior. The window was full of a mixture of neon signs, flyers, and advertising. The neon said things like, PIERCING $25 or TATTOO, but most promising was OPEN.

Will closed the door on the Camry, walked around the vehicle, and stepping ahead of his brother, opened the door to the shop.

\* \* \*

A bell chimed with the door, and though Will didn't jump, the noise made him tense. There was a glass countertop full of jewelry directly in front of him, and behind that was a skinny girl whose arms looked as though they'd seen a few practice sessions. She had the grayish pallor that tends to suggest a history with either heroin or time served, if not both. There was a scarab tattooed on her throat, and Will stared at the dancing bug as she said, "Can I help you with something?" There was no mistaking the irritation in her voice.

It wasn't like Will and Isaac were dressed well, and the car wasn't a showpiece by any means, but still, it was obvious this wasn't a world they belonged to anymore, if they ever had. *This is what happens if you keep fucking up and none of your friends shoots you*, thought Will.

Smiling at the girl, he said, "We're here to talk to Jason."

"Yeah? Do you have an appointment?"

"No. I'm an old friend."

"Acquaintance," interjected Isaac. "We knew him a long time ago. It's been a while."

She didn't care enough to respond beyond sliding off her stool and walking into the back. A stereo clicked on playing AC/DC, and the girl returned a couple minutes later.

"Sorry, no dice. Says he's busy."

"Tell him Will Daniels is here to talk to him."

She sighed. "Is that name going to mean anything to him? 'Cause he gets mad pretty easy, and he's got a bad hangover. Might be you want to make an appointment, hope for the best."

"Tell him Will Daniels is here to talk to him."

She smirked at him. "If that's your hard look, you might want to work on getting a new one. I'm going to ask one more time, and when I come back and tell you he said to fuck off, you two are going to fuck off."

She disappeared into the back of the store again and was back faster this time.

"Jason says to come on back." She was smiling, and his stomach dropped to his feet. Will's bravado had been stripped clean by her Sicilian smile, and the pistol under his coat may as well have been back at the house for all the good it would do him should he fumble to retrieve it.

She led them down a short hallway that had a door on either side of it and another one at the end. They walked through the door on the right, and the girl left them in the room, closing the door behind her as she left.

Sitting on a stool was Jason. Next to him, on a steel cart, were a pair of tattoo guns, and next to them was a different kind of gun, a revolver. Will stared at it with a lump in his throat before turning his attention back to Jason.

His old friend had a stomach that was stretching his shirt taut, the kind of belly earned by cheap food and cheaper booze. He had on an American flag bandanna, and coming out of the bottom of the back of it was a gray braid that lay over his right shoulder and hung almost to his belly. His arms, hands, and neck were covered in tattoos, gray ones that looked like the kind from prison and colored ones that looked like the kind that weren't. His ears bore two large hoops, silver and thick as pencils, each holding silver beads at its center.

Jason did not stand when they entered, nor did he offer them a seat. "Will Daniels," he said. "And is that your brother with you? Older, right? I don't recognize you, but the same family is in both faces."

Will thought about that statement, his eyes poring over Jason's familiar and yet foreign face.

"Yeah," said Isaac, "I'm his brother." He extended a hand and said, "Name's I—"

"I don't give a ruddy fuck what your name is," said Jason. "I'm curious about why in the fuck you're here, and once I figure out why, I'm going to run you out of my fucking shop, all right? I have a feeling I'm going to be amused for about thirty seconds, tops." He turned his attention back to Will. "C'mon, *William*. Spit it out, author-boy. Why are you slumming with your old buddy?"

Will was taken aback. Jason had obviously made some effort to follow his life. His books had sold well, but not that well. Yet Jason knew enough to know he'd published them under *William Daniels*, not *Will*.

Will collected himself as best he was able and got on with it. "I'm here to talk to you about my son."

"Bad start, Will. I'm already bored."

"My son was killed a little less than a week ago after being involved in a bank robbery."

"All right, I think I know the one," said Jason, who winked at him. "Much better start. Now I'm interested."

"He was killed in an abandoned barn, shot in the head, and then burned to death with some of the evidence."

"No honor among thieves, right, Will? That's nothing new there, just how it is. Like when I got penned up and you walked. Just how it is."

There it was. "I wasn't there when you got busted."

"You were there enough other times," Jason growled. "And we were *expecting* you that night. Waited for you, even, until I said we needed to get on with it."

"I was tired of doing that stuff. Just dumb luck I wasn't there, nothing more."

"Dumb luck."

It was all Will could do to hold the man's gaze, but he knew he damn well better. "Lucky, lucky you. You might be the luckiest fucker I know, *William*."

"Look," said Will, "I'm here to ask you to help me find the men who killed my son."

There followed a long, long moment in which Will fell into the blackness of the other man's eyes and spun down and down in it. It was fine with him. It matched his own blackness, and he found he didn't mind the company.

It was Jason who pulled out first. "Will, listen to me," he said, "and then get the fuck out of here. Even if I could help you find the men who killed your son, I wouldn't. You know why? You're not the type for that kind of work. I mean, really, what are you going to do, ask them for a fucking apology? I can see you've got a gun in your shirt right now, and it's just fucking ridiculous on you. You need to get the fuck out of here and forget that this conversation ever happened, all right? Just take your brother and go back to your little house, maybe add this to one of your stories and tell your faggot writer friends about how involved you get in your writing. Either the police will catch them or not. They probably won't, and that'll be that."

"I need you to help me find the men who killed my son," Will said, "and you're going to do it."

Jason's eyebrows lifted. "Will," he said, "this is no longer funny, do you understand? I can be a nice enough guy, under the right circumstances, but this ain't them, and you ain't a friend. Last chance. Get. The. Fuck. Out."

"You're going to help me find the men who killed my son," said Will, and as he spoke the words, Jason stood from his stool, a sawn-off baseball bat appearing in his right hand like a magic trick. Isaac was grabbing Will's shoulder, but Will continued. "You're going to help me find them, because my son could just as easily have had your blood in him as mine."

**❝W**hat the fuck did you just say?❞ Jason said. The color hadn't quite drained from his face, but all the deadly ease in it had disappeared. "The *fuck*?"

"Will?" It was Isaac, beside him. Will hadn't thought about him in what felt like an hour. "What in the hell are you talking about?"

Jason sat back in his stool, and Will grabbed a folding chair leaning against the wall, unfolded it, and sat. Isaac, looking confused, finally decided to do the same.

"I said that my son Alex could just as easily be your blood as mine."

"Explain. And if you're fucking with me, this is going to be a lot worse. I can take getting fucked with a little, but not like that and definitely not from you, not ever."

"You used to go around with Patty Edwards, right?"

"Yeah, before I got sent up. I fucked her here and there, never my squeeze, but a sidepiece."

"Yeah, I used to go around with her too. As far as I know, though, we were it. Fire and ice, or something like it—she wanted the guy who seemed like he might make it out of the life and the dude who would kick in the door. I used to think I was running a scam on her, being with her and then other chicks when she wasn't around."

"So did I," said Jason, "but she had her own shit going on too, huh?"

"Exactly. She was running her own little show, but like I said, we were it."

"And Patty's your son's mother," Jason said. "How come I didn't know that?"

"You were in the can, and when you got out, she was gone."

Jason nodded, taking it in. "And when I got out, you had a kid you were raising. I guess I did know that, not that I gave a shit. By then you were dead to me, and lucky you weren't dead to you too." He shook his head. "Patty's kid. Fuck me running."

"Why is this a surprise to me too?" Isaac asked, but Will ignored his brother.

"Yep, Patty was his deadbeat mom. She skipped town three days after having him, and I never heard from her again."

"She got beat to death in a truck stop parking lot," Jason said. "Working as a lot lizard ended up not agreeing with her."

"How long ago?" Will asked. "How could I not know about this?"

"That's ancient history, buddy. She died at least ten years ago, crapped out at least one other kid, as far as I know. I got to admit, that part didn't interest me too much. Didn't make much of a splash, though, at least not here. In South Dakota, she was what most people referred to as number fifteen—as in, the fifteenth hooker to get skull-fucked by some asshole blowing through town. Last I checked, they still hadn't caught the guy."

"Jesus Christ."

"I don't figure they're looking at him for it, but I'll pass the word along—if I happen across the right people, of course." Jason made a cigarette appear from a pack on the bottom shelf of his cart and lit it with a match he ignited on the bottom of an engineer boot. "So, anyways, let's hear the rest of it."

"Patty came to my mom, dropped off the kid in her lap, and skipped town. I was out drinking, wondering what the fuck was ever going to happen with my shitty life. When I came home—boom—time to play house."

"And I was sitting in stir."

"Exactly. Patty told my mother the story about the kid either being yours or mine too. My mom's the only one besides me—well, *us* now, I suppose—that ever knew the truth."

"Do you have a picture?"

Will took his phone from his pocket—slowly, so as not to alarm Jason—and turned it on. He went to the pictures app and found one of a smiling Alex from nearly ten years ago, dressed in a baseball uniform. Will gave the picture a look, wondering not for the last time just what in the hell had gone wrong with his boy, and handed the phone to Jason.

"Cute little fucker. Takes after his mother. To be honest, I don't see a bit of either one us on his mug."

"Yeah, I never did, either. I've lost more than one night thinking about it, though. He was a tough kid to raise, I can tell you. Damn near put my wife in the loony bin. Between my drinking and his wild streak, she's had some hard times."

"Hard times make hard people. So how did your son get hooked up with such a rotten bunch? My memory is a little fuzzy when it comes to the details of the robbery, but I do know a bunch of people got toe tags over it."

"Yes. Alex killed one of them. I never thought he had that in him. I know I never did."

Jason shrugged. "Well, maybe an apple don't have to be close to a tree to still fall off a branch."

"What do you mean?"

"If the kid had my blood, could explain a lot about his mean streak. I was never much of one to listen to reason, and I've done some things in my time when I was forced to."

The two of them were quiet for a long minute, staring off at nothing.

Will pulled out of it first. "Will you help us find out who did this?"

Jason scowled at him, then sank back down into himself again. When he came out of it this time, he was nodding. "Yeah.

I know I'm going to regret it, but I'll help. Just keep in mind, the answers you get may not be the answers you want. Chances are this is going to end with us up popping a couple of hopheads, likely won't be much different than shooting a rabid pooch. What's your phone number?"

Will told him, and Jason punched it into his phone.

"Listen, if I have any news worth sharing, I'm going to call you from a burner cell phone, a throwaway. I'll tell you we need to meet, and we're going to get together at Founder's Brewery that same day, at nine p.m. Don't ask me what I found or anything else. If I call you from the tattoo shop phone—ends in five-zero-nine-two—that means I either found nothing or opened a wormhole too deep for us to do anything about. That sound all right with you?"

"Sounds fine. Thanks."

"I'm not going to say it's no problem, but I'm glad you got a hold of me. Whether that kid was my blood or not doesn't matter. I'll do this for Patty."

saac's hands were white on the wheel of the Camry. The weather had to be a part of it—blowing snow was turning into a full-on blizzard, and the visibility was extremely low. Still, the Camry handled in a sure-footed way as they meandered onto the highway, where traffic was chugging along at a brisk thirty miles per hour.

"Were you ever going to tell me?" Isaac asked. "Did anyone know besides Mom?"

"No. I was never going to tell you, because it didn't matter to me. He was my son, whether he was my blood or not. That's why I never did a paternity test, and that's why I still wouldn't do one now. I don't need blood to tell me about family or about being a father to a little boy that has nothing. I was just a kid when Patty left him with us, and he made me grow up a lot. Not to say I wasn't still a fuckup, but I was less of one." He looked away. "I guess less wasn't good enough for Alex," he said to the passenger-side window.

"Do you really believe that if Jason is his blood father, that maybe that's why Alex took the thing to the next level?" Isaac asked. "Or do you think it's just some bizarre coincidence?"

Will shrugged.

Isaac nodded to himself, working it over in his head. "I guess I've never believed in genetics like that—that it would make someone more likely to commit murder or other violent crimes. But this might be changing my mind a little bit. Are you sure you don't want to get a paternity test?"

"Listen. I just know that someone killed my son, and I want to know why. The rest of the testing, the blood relations, genetics—none of it matters to me. I never would have told Jason about this when Alex was alive and never would have after he was dead unless I had too. I think I made the right decision."

"What if Jason finds—fuck!" A big-assed pickup had fishtailed around them. "These roads suck, and that guy is doing like fifty!" Isaac shook his head, then settled down and went back to what he'd started. "So what if Jason finds out who did this, gets an address or something?"

"I've been thinking a lot about that, and I keep coming back to the same thing. If I find out who killed my son and it wasn't for a damn good reason, I'm going to kill him. It would just need doing. If the cops can't catch these guys, they'll do it again, and someone else will get hurt."

Will felt Isaac looking at him, but kept his eyes straight ahead.

"That's pretty heavy, Will. I want to say I'll see this through with you, but I'm not sure that I can. I mean, I have a life too. A wife. And my priors are old, but when they can show a history of criminal behavior, and you've got shit on your record, that's not good."

"You can do what you want. I asked you to come along so I had backup with Jason, but if you don't feel like seeing this through is right for you, I understand. It would be a lot to ask, especially of a brother who I basically ignore and who basically ignores me." Will grinned. "It's a lot to ask of anybody."

"Shit," said Isaac, "we still have to get groceries."

\* \* \*

The storm had gotten worse in the time they'd spent in the store. With the parking lot's slush and ice gumming its wheels, the cart was reduced to a very awkward sleigh. When they finally reached the car, they threw the groceries into the trunk, any care over the condition of bread or eggs beaten out of them by a desperate desire to escape the deluge of heavy, wet snow.

Trunk loaded, cart placed in the corral, they dove inside, and Isaac began to slowly steer them from the parking lot. The ringing of Will's phone broke the brothers' concentrated silence, and Will saw that it was Alison.

"Hey, babe," he said. "We're on our way. Come up with something else you need us to get?"

"No. How are the roads?" Alison's voice was muffled, riddled with static.

"Really bad."

"Well, don't hurry home, but get here. The news just said the mall was closed. That means that's its officially graduated to really fucking nasty out."

"I believe it. This is like twenty eleven all over again."

"Don't even say that, mister. That was horrible. We've got enough on our plate without a full-blown blizzard."

"Yeah well, I think that's what we've got. I'm going to let you go. We'll see you soon. Only, probably not too soon."

"Tell your brother to drive safe."

"No need, he is."

"Tell him from me."

Will hung up the phone. "She says not to kill us."

"Check."

The wind was moving the snow fast enough that they could see drifts appearing out of nowhere, using a tree or the side of a building to take root and form into massive piles.

"You doing OK?" Will asked.

"I'm still driving."

"I mean with everything else."

"No, Will, not really. Sorry for that, but I'm being honest."

"I said I'd understand if you didn't want to go on from here."

He gave his head a shake. "I'm not talking about that. I'm talking about you signing on with Jason. That fucker—he should have been tried for rape in that last B and E when he got busted, remember?"

"Yeah."

"And what happened there?"

"He never got charged with it."

"You're missing the point. The girl refused to testify, and there wasn't enough evidence beyond what she told the police initially. It never occurred to you that he might have threatened her family?"

"No. I don't know. I didn't exactly follow what happened to him. To any of them. I had my own life to worry about, and then I had Alex."

In front of them, the wind shoved a GMC Denali right off of the road. The big truck was catching enough wind on its large frame that its four-wheel drive had ceased to matter, and the thing slid horizontally off the highway as though moved by a god.

"Jesus," Will said, "did you see that? That's fucking nuts."

"They're going to be waiting for a wrecker for a while too. Anyways, though, like I was saying, there's a reason Jason served the maximum possible sentence for that B and E, and his time had nothing to do with a little smash-and-grab. He made a sixteen-year-old girl blow him, and when it came down to her word against his, she decided not to talk."

"None of that matters now. He did his time, and he's the only person who can help me find out who hurt Alex. If that gets a little blood under my fingernails, then so be it."

Isaac shook his head and went back to watching the road. Vehicles were pulled over and stuck on roadside culverts as they traveled. When the two brothers pulled off the highway, they both let out sighs of relief.

T wo days after the worst of the blizzard, the plow trucks
were clearing and salting the streets, the sun was shining
and suggesting winter might finally be coming to a close, and
Will received three phone calls. The first was from Lou.

"How you holding up, buddy?" Lou exclaimed into the
phone, before Will could even say hello.

"I'm doing OK. Alison seems to be getting better as well. I
think my brother is going home pretty soon too, now that he
can. I know he meant to only be here for a day or two, but the
snow had other plans. Plus, I think he's enjoying the little vacay
from work and his old lady." Isaac was sitting across the kitchen
table from Will as he spoke and flipped his little brother a middle
finger and a grin.

"That's great, great stuff. Any word from the law? Have they
said if they have any leads?"

"Nope. Nothing on releasing Alex's body, either."

"I already told you this, but I can start making waves on that,
light a fire under their asses."

"No. I'm sure it's just the snow. It slowed down everything
else, may as well slow down the cops and the medical examiner
too. I'll let you know if I change my mind." After a beat, Will
said, "Lou, I know you aren't just calling to see how I am."

"I'm like a piece of glass," Lou said. "There's a window into
my soul, what can I say? The people at Fox want to talk to you.
Might score some national coverage, give you a chance to tell

your side. Alison could be on if she wanted to as well—hell, that's what they want—but I told them I'd talk to you."

"I don't know."

"Will, these people put you on the air twice when you were promoting books. I'll get a list of questions beforehand, and it won't be live—it's pretty much best-case scenario. You get to tell your story in a safe setting, and if stuff goes badly, we have them edit the hell out of it."

"Give me a day to talk to Alison, but you can tell them I'll do it—once I approve those questions, of course."

"Great! They're going to be thrilled. I'm going to get on the horn with them. I'll get back to you soon—day or two, tops."

The phone clicked off, but before Will could replace it in the pocket of his jeans, it began to ring again. *Christ, what now?* Checking the caller ID, Will could see that it was a 206 area code. *Jack, most likely.*

"Hello?"

"Hey, Will, do you have a couple of minutes?"

"Yeah, sure. What's going on, Jack?" Will stood from the kitchen table, held a finger up to his brother to say, *One minute,* and then walked into the dining room.

"I was able to talk to Terri and Bruce this morning. Don't freak out, but we had a meeting to discuss your issues. Actually, before I say anything else, it's all good news, so really don't freak out."

"I'm good."

"Cool. Terri and Bruce both agreed with me that we should push your next title back a little bit, maybe a quarter or two from when you normally release, so nothing crazy. I think they would have gone for it either way, but I sort of gave a nudge in that direction, and they went for it. I didn't mention that you weren't writing right now. I mean, I assume they would think you weren't writing because of what happened, but I didn't say you were kind of stonewalled before that.

"Here's where it gets really good. Terri still wants you to get something to her when you normally do, but we'll have a ton more time to work out the kinks. If you get in by the middle of summer, you'd most likely be looking at a fall release next year. I think that should be totally doable, writer's block or not, and it should give you a way to escape from reality for a bit.

"The other great part is that if the next book is as good as your first two, Terri will likely negotiate an advance with you. Now, don't quote me on that part, but we all feel terrible about what happened, and none of us want it to affect your ability to produce new work, or need to take time away from doing what you love, for something that isn't your fault."

"I appreciate that, Jack. And the possibility of an advance—that's awesome."

"Will, we want you to do well. This is enough to go through, not to mention writing. That said, dude, you need to give us something we can work with. You need to produce something awesome, something that works within the genre that you found success in. We both know you can write, but you need to stay focused. I loved that last thing, but it was way off the reservation in terms of what people have come to expect from you."

"I got that, Jack. Once this is a little more settled, I'll get back to the keyboard."

"Good, that makes me super happy. Get through this, and get to writing. You've done it before; you'll do it again. Just because the last one was a no-go doesn't mean we don't want more from you or that some crazy Norse god took all your stories away. You're a good writer, and writers write."

"Thanks, Jack, for everything. I can't say that enough. I'll let you know when this is over."

Will hung up the phone, trying to flush the tears from his eyes. Jack was 100 percent correct. It was time to get back to the keyboard and, instead of whining about writer's block, to start telling stories. He'd picked writing as a way to get out of a dead end of a job—and dead end for a life—and to throw away everything he'd accomplished wasn't only unreasonable, it was childish. The phone ringing a third time interrupted his thoughts and made him almost throw the thing to the floor.

Will didn't recognize the number and almost ignored the call. Then he remembered what Jason had said about calling on a burner, a throwaway cell with a number he wouldn't recognize.

"Hello?"

"Meet me tonight. Bring what you brought the other day."

Jason hung up before Will could even attempt a response, and it wasn't until the phone was back in his pocket that he realized Jason had meant for him to bring a gun.

\* \* \*

"Isaac, I need to talk to Alison for a few minutes."

Isaac stood. His brother had gone pale, and before he could disguise it, Alison saw him.

Turning to Will, he could tell that she had been waiting all along for the other shoe to drop. "Is it bad news?" she asked as Isaac fled to the basement. "I'm not sure I can take much more of that. I suppose you'll tell me either way, though."

"This is good news and bad news," said Will. "Mostly good, but a little bad—at least you may think so. I talked to Jack. It looks like there will be a delay on my next book, once I get around to writing, editing, and submitting it, of course. It sounds like they want to avoid any negative publicity that Alex's…situation could send my way."

"That sounds OK. Right?"

"Except, I have no idea who or what I'll be writing about." Will considered telling her about the possible advance, finally deciding against it. It would be better not to play with her feelings over something that might not happen. "But none of that matters. They still want to see work from me and, if it's up to snuff, promote and publish it. If anything, the delay is a good thing. It will give me time to write and really play with what I want my third book to be. I have to imagine that *Bottles* sold enough that there will be people out there actually expecting something from the next Will Daniels book, as weird as that is to actually come right out and say."

"That all sounds great, Will. And of course people are waiting for your next one."

"The other thing, though, it's not as pleasant."

The light that had risen in her eyes went out, just like that, and he wondered if anything that he might have to do in the following weeks, days, or even hours could be forgiven.

"Isaac and I went and met up with an old friend on that grocery trip during the blizzard the other day. He's a friend from when I was still trouble—or at least thought I was trouble. This guy, though, he was the real deal then, and he still is now. I asked him if he could get me any information on who had hurt Alex, and he said he would call if he was able to. We already had a set time and place to meet, so all he had to do was call on the day he wanted to meet if he had any information."

"And he called you."

"Yes, he did."

"So what are you going to do?"

"I'm going to meet with him, and I'm hoping Isaac will come with me."

"I know you're going to meet with him—I'm not an idiot. It's obvious you're set to go do something. I mean, if he can get you info and show you who hurt Alex, *then* what are you going to do?"

"I don't know yet. I suppose I'd want to turn them into the police, but I'm not sure that would even be an option. I know that Wixom—the guy who's helping us—would never have gotten involved if there were even a possibility of police involvement."

"Will, do think the police are going to catch the men who killed our son?"

"No. Do you?"

"No, I don't. That makes me feel very weak and also very scared, but I don't think they will. I think that, even if they do, it will be an accident."

They thought about that together, eyes locked, and then she said, "I guess what I mean is, I want you to be safe. And I don't want you to do anything you'll regret every time you close your eyes. But"—she swallowed, and steel came into her eyes—"I want those men punished. If that means that you and your brother need to call every old hood that you know from some long-buried little black book, you do it. Those men killed my son."

**W**ill and Isaac sat at Founders. Will was drinking a glass of Breakfast Stout, and Isaac was too. Both brothers were nervous, but only Isaac had admitted to it on the car ride over to the brewery.

The Sig felt heavy in Will's jacket, but not like it had when they'd gone to Jason's tattoo shop. If anything, it felt like a keyboard to a writer or a hammer to a carpenter. It was a tool necessary for the right sort of job. Isaac was carrying as well, a small 9mm that Will had picked up as a summer carry piece, if he ever got around to taking a concealed carry class.

They were at a table near the rear of the brewery, figuring that Jason would be able to find them even if they tried to hide from him. The building itself was packed. Most of the tables, about twenty in all, were occupied, and the fifty-seat bar had nary a single empty stool. Conversations roared, and Will understood why Jason had picked this place, even if it seemed like the last sort of bar that he would ever hang out in on his own. It was perfect. With the varied tables of oddly mixed groups, they wouldn't stand out in the least.

Jason appeared out of nowhere. He just sat at their table with a pint of a beer that was dark, though not as dark as their own.

"Dirty Bastard," he said. "The beer, not you two fucks. Never had it, but it sounds about right, considering circumstances." He took a long pull from the glass, draining half of it, and then placed it on the table. "How're things, gents?"

"Lovely," said Will. "What have you got for us?"

"Don't be a fucking idiot," Jason said, wearing a smile like he'd just met with two old friends. "I can't fucking tell you right here. You see those two assholes over there?" Jason nodded at two hipsterish kids standing in a glassed-in box just outside of the bar. One of them had horn-rimmed glasses, a handlebar mustache, and a worn messenger bag with an Apple patch sewn onto it. The other looked about the same, just different affectations, a fedora, vest, and neon-green scarf. Both men were texting on iPhones.

"I see them."

"Well, when they finish their smokes, we're going to saunter on over there into the smoke-box so my good buddies won't let me get lonely while I puff on a butt. Sound good?"

Will and Isaac both nodded, and all three men drank from their glasses of beer. The beer was good and made Will's head hum a little, but he didn't feel the urge to consume vast sums of it, either. As if on cue, the hipsters left the smoking area, and Will, Isaac, and Jason left their beers on the table to walk to the room. Will held the door open for his brother and his old friend and then followed them in.

"OK, this is going to be short and sweet," said Jason. "I got a name, this fuck who likes young pussy, guy named Mumbo. Fat Hispanic kid."

"What kind of name is Mumbo?" Isaac asked. "That's seriously weird."

"It's the kind of name that either a junkie whore mother gives you or one of your buddies give you. Does it fucking matter? Guy goes by Mumbo, and I know for a fucking fact that he was there."

An electric hum had kicked up in Will, and Jason eyed him like he could see it. "Now, don't get crazy thoughts going. I don't know if he was the one that aced your boy, or if he even knew that was part of the plan when it happened. Maybe you both have forgotten, but things can change on a job."

"Like getting sucked off by a sixteen-year-old?" Isaac said.

The little glass room took on a different hum then. They all took turns looking at each other. Will imagined blood splattering the glass. Buckets of it.

Isaac spoke first, his voice hoarse and quiet, like he couldn't quite believe he'd blurted that out. "C'mon, Will," he said, "let's get out of here before we can't."

"That," said Jason, smoke flowing from his nostrils, "is what they call 'one.' You just got your all-time fill of taking digs at me. You do it again, I will fucking beat you to death, right here in front of all of these nice people. I can't see any of them stopping me or stopping me leaving when I'm done. I'll be back in my shop with some pal in my chair in fifteen minutes, and if anybody asks, I'll have been there all evening."

"We're fine, Jason," said Will. "What's the plan?"

Jason drew in another long, slow lungful of smoke, still looking at Isaac like he was cataloging the various abuses he would be visiting upon him. Then he exhaled and said, "I'm going to finish my smoke, then we're going to go in, finish our beers, and Isaac is going to settle our tabs." He turned a sweet smile on Isaac. "Don't say shit, brother. Remember, you already got your one." To both of them, he said, "After that, we're going to go to Mumbo's in whatever car you two took here, and we're going to ask him some questions. His answers will tell us what to do next."

"You mean, where to go?"

"No, to decide if he's got anything to tell us first or if we just kill him right away."

saac drove, Will sat next to him, and Jason was crammed into the backseat. Will had offered his seat up front to Jason, but he'd just smiled and declined. Now, with an almost certainly armed man with a black past sitting behind him, Will understood the decision. Not that he could imagine why Jason would have any reason to fear them. It was probably just habit, like how old west gunslingers never sat with their backs to a doorway.

They were silent in the car, with Jason giving occasional directions. He had them staying off the highway and moving into the southwest side of the city, far from the robbery, at least as far as Grand Rapids was concerned, but really only about a twenty-minute car ride.

Jason directed them onto a side street off of Ivanrest, which led them to the type of unidentifiable neighborhood that littered Kent County. Only the cars—half fancy, half rolling rust—were proof that it had been turned from a thriving suburb to a near ghetto of foreclosed-upon houses turned to rental properties.

"Stop here," said Jason, and Isaac did. Jason handed the brothers leather gloves and put on a pair himself. Will exited the car first, with Jason after him. After a moment, Isaac followed. Jason walked to the back of the car, and Will watched him grab a handful of wet snow and smash it onto Isaac's license plate. When he was finished, Jason walked from the car and nodded toward a house.

"That one," he said; it was a nondescript house with white aluminum siding. The house could have used some work but

74

wasn't nearly as bad off as some of the other ones in the neighborhood. There was an old Ford truck parked in the driveway. Will had only a fleeting moment to wonder just how sure Jason was about this being the right house before he was following his friend across the street, with Isaac at his heels. Jason had a pistol in his gloved hand, not the revolver from the tattoo shop, some sort of smaller automatic that Will didn't recognize.

The night was pitch-black, the only light coming from houses and the moon, and the snow picked up all of it, casting it in odd reflections. There were the sounds of their feet, automobiles streets away, and the call and response of suburbia, one dog barking, another howling, back and forth. Will noticed all of it and none of it, his world running black and red between fear and anger.

When Will's feet hit the driveway, he took the Sig from its place in the holster but kept it close to his body. Jason walked to the door. Will was readying himself, waiting for him to knock or ring the buzzer, when Jason kicked the door in and barreled into the house, his pistol up. Fighting every instinct that he'd forced onto himself over the past twenty-odd years, Will followed him, his adrenaline like nothing he'd experienced since he was a teenager.

The first thing Will saw was Jason holding his pistol on a soft man on a couch with his hands high in the air. The man, who looked like he was still covered in baby fat, was wearing a headset hooked to an Xbox 360 controller; he had been playing some war game, a shooter. On the coffee table in front of him was a half-finished forty of Mickey's malt liquor, a smoldering blue translucent bong, a soft pack of Camel Lights, an overflowing ashtray, a plate with half of a sandwich on it, a bottle of throat spray, Zicam, cough drops, and three thick stacks of banded fifty-dollar bills.

The man winced when Jason tore the headphones from his ears. Isaac heaving the door closed behind them was thunder in the room, the only other noise coming from the television.

"Are you Mumbo, you cunt?" Jason asked the man, and the fat man was nodding, Will realizing as he did so that one of his raised hands was still holding the 360 controller, the headphones dangling from it. "I asked you a question," said Jason. "Yes or no. Are you Mumbo?"

The man tried to speak, but failed the first time. He tried again, this time managing a torn-sounding "Yes."

"You have exactly no lies left," said Jason, pushing his pistol into Mumbo's face. "Is there anyone else here?"

"No."

"Anyone coming soon?"

"No."

"Perfect, we have some things to discuss."

T he television was turned up loud—still just Mumbo's game, but roaring with war sounds now. Luckily, most of those sounds were gunshots and swearing.

Mumbo's wrists were bound with strips from the shirt Jason had torn off him. His ankles were bound as well, those to a chair Jason had taken from the kitchen. Atop the chair's seat, and under Mumbo's fat ass, was a plastic bowl that Jason had also found in the kitchen. He had shoved three steak knives down through the bottom of it, then flipped the bowl upside down. The more Mumbo's weight pushed down on the upside-down bowl, the more the bowl flattened, and the deeper the knives went into Mumbo.

Mumbo's ass was bleeding, and the blood was pooling slowly under the chair. His mouth had been stuffed with what was left of his shirt, and the big man was crying.

Will felt sick over what was happening, but kept reminding himself that Alex was dead and this man had been a part of that death. He concentrated on his job. Will held Mumbo's Xbox controller, his finger on the right trigger button. Jason had told him that if Mumbo started yelling, he was to pull that trigger and make the TV loud.

Jason sat in a chair opposite Mumbo. Jason's gun was resting on his knee, and Will stood behind him. Isaac was still waiting in the doorway.

At last, Jason gave a look to his watch and said, "All right, that's ten minutes." He stood and stepped to Mumbo, which made the big man begin to twitch with fear. But rather than further terrorizing the man, Jason had Will join him, and together, they eased Mumbo and his chair back onto the floor. The points of the blades still stuck to him, but the bowl was lifted from the seat of the chair, and Will watched Mumbo's eyes loll as the pain began to dissipate.

"All right," said Jason as he removed Mumbo's gag, "I told you one rule already, so you know not to lie. Here's rule number two. Do not fucking speak unless spoken to. Rule number three, if you get loud, you will die badly." Jason stood, leaving Mumbo lying on the floor and stuck to the chair. "One last thing, all right, buddy? There is a bonus round, assuming you play nice in the opening ones. I'm not going to make any promises on that, though. Are you ready?"

"Yes," said Mumbo in his wrecked voice.

"Nasty throat you've got there, buddy," Wixom said. "Remember rule one, now. That's not just a cold, is it?"

Mumbo just looked at him.

"Gasoline fire, I'm guessing," Jason said. "Hurts like a fucker, doesn't it? Makes the throat raw. Beyond raw, if you're close when it goes up. Makes it feel like running a comb through hot pizza. It's a fucking wreck. You been near a gas fire recently, Mumbo?"

The big man shook his head, and Jason shook his own head back. As Will watched, Jason kicked the upturned bottom of the chair as hard as he could, forcing the plastic bowl against the seat and the bowl with its attached knives into Mumbo. Will pulled the trigger, and what California had decided a .50-caliber gun fired in the desert sounded like roared through and over the scream.

"Shit," said Jason, "that is no way to enter a bonus round. It is a surefire violation of rule numero uno and is going to make me have to challenge everything else you say." Jason grabbed the bowl and forced the chair away from Mumbo again, using the bowl as a handle. Will pulled the trigger again, and pretend gunfire roared through the very real battlefield inside of the house while Mumbo whimpered and the knives slid out.

"Damn," said Jason, "we are off to a bad start. Last question again, were you recently around a gas fire that burned the fuck out of your throat?"

"Yes," Mumbo squeaked.

"Were you recently involved in a robbery, keeping in mind I can still see the fucking stacks on the table?"

"Yes."

"Did you kill someone during that robbery?"

"Yeah, man, I did," sputtered Mumbo, blood pooling on the floor under him. "They hired you guys, didn't they? Someone who knew that little girl that died, right? I shot the fuck out of that place. Chris said it wasn't a regular one, that we should make it memorable. I didn't know I smoked a kid until we got home."

"I do not give a fuck about a little kid. Do you believe me?"

"Yes."

"Was there a man with you named Alex during that robbery?"

"Yes."

"Good answer, Mumbo. Did you kill him?"

"No."

"Last chance to avoid a really bad death. I'm thinking I hate your clavicles. Did you kill him?"

"No," said Mumbo, and he began to weep. "We were friends."

"So who fucking killed him then?"

"Chris did," said Mumbo. "Chris killed him, and it made no sense at all—at least not to me."

"Fine," said Jason. "I want you to tell me everything about Alex dying." Jason nudged the chair back toward Mumbo, Will pulling the trigger on the 360 controller again as Mumbo screamed, even though the knives were inches from his ass. "Seriously, buddy, tell me everything. Shit, be selfish. Do it for you. You have no friends left in this world, Mumbo."

"It was supposed to be simple," Mumbo said, blubbering but visibly trying to calm himself. "Chris called me and said we had a job to do. I was happy; I'd blown through all of the money we made on the last one—well, almost all of it. Do you want to know about the last one?"

"No," Will said, surprising himself by talking. "We want to know about this one. When did Chris call you?"

"I don't know, a week before we did the job?"

"Go on," Jason said. "What happened next?"

"Shit," Mumbo said, "nothing. Like I said, Chris told me he wanted me for a job and that our friend Rob was going to drive— he's done that for us before—and that Alex was going to be there too. I didn't hear from Chris again until the day before we pulled the job on that bank. Him, Alex, and Rob just showed up like it was no big thing. Chris gave me this little AK that he said he wanted me to use on the job, and I said something like, 'Isn't that a little much?' but Chris said no, the fence wanted a sure thing, better too much gun than too little, I guess. Usually, they say a shooting on a job like that gets so much heat that they want nothing to do with the shit you stole in the first place, but I didn't hear none of that. We didn't really talk much about it, though. Rob had a bunch of weed, and we just sat here, man, drinking and smoking, passing out and waking up. We ate some breakfast at IHOP and then rolled to the job.

"Everything went good in the bank, I guess. Or the way it was supposed to, I mean. I'm not a hard-ass like Chris. I've killed people before, but I never really wanted to, you know? Chris had seen us all kill people before, though—"

"Hold on," Will said, all three sets of eyes in the room turning to him. "You're saying Alex was a murderer?"

"Shit yes," said Mumbo. "Chris had him kill one of my regular pieces of ass because Chris was tweaked on meth and thought she might be snitching. Dee was a good lay, too; that was a waste. We even turned her out on the bank manager too. Shit, killing her was a total bummer. Chris had Alex kill her with the same gun that he killed Alex with."

Will could feel the blood rushing through his eardrums, and he steadied himself. The girl Alex had murdered was the one Van Endel had told him about, Cassidy, the sixteen-year-old killed with that shotgun pistol, the Judge.

"How do I know you're telling the truth?" Will said. "How do I know you didn't kill her?"

"I am *not* going to lie," said Mumbo, using his eyes to indicate Jason. "I'd tell you if I did. I killed the kid in the bank, I told you that! I'd tell you."

"Enough of this shit," said Jason. "Fill in the rest of the blanks."

Mumbo was telling the truth. Alex had murdered a young girl for no reason other than that he was told to.

"OK," Mumbo said. "So we get up, get our shit together—you know, 'lock and load,' all that movie shit. We drive out there, me and Chris in the back of the van, Alex and Rob up front. Chris was telling us the details again, which we were all fucking sick of hearing. 'Do the job, get paper, get the fuck out. Rob's the driver, I'm the guard, Chris and Alex are going in the vault. The manager is in on it; when he leaves, that's the sign to go in.' Over and over, he's saying this shit, man. It was boring."

"Did anything go sideways in the bank?" Jason asked, and Mumbo shook his head.

"What, other than putting lead to so many people for no fucking reason? That was a little sideways. But they were screaming and freaking out after Alex shot one of the suit dudes, and one thing led to another, and fast.

"After Chris and Alex came out of the vault, Rob pulled the truck around, and we went to the drop. Chris, Rob, and Alex had been there a bunch of times, but I hadn't. It was an old farm, with a barn that looked like a stiff breeze would knock over. They'd stashed another car there so we could ditch the van. Cops are dumb, you know? They hear about a van, it's all they can think about for like ten hours. Like, when you see one of those amber alerts for some kidnapped baby. All a nigga has to do is switch cars, and he's good for like a day.

"Anyways, we do the job, get back to the barn, and we're taking the bags of money from the van to the car. Alex said something to Chris—I couldn't hear what—and then Chris shot him. It was loud as fuck. I come out the van thinking the law was coming in, I got my AK up, and Chris is just standing over Alex, and like, half of Alex's head is just gone. Me and Rob are standing on either side of Chris, like, 'What the fuck?' and he just told us to keep moving the shit. When we were done, Rob pulled the car out, and Chris and I covered Alex and the van with gas. I was a little close when it went up, fire sucked the lungs right out of my chest."

"That's a damn good job, Mumbo," said Jason, "but these next few questions are very, very important. I want short, to-the-point answers. And telling me that you don't know where somebody lives or that you'll have to show us, that's not going to work, not today."

"I know that by now. I'll be as straight as I can."

"Are Chris and Rob both still alive?"

"As far as I know. They were both here last night."

"Where does Rob live?"

"About five miles from here. He's off of Ivanrest too."

Mumbo told them the address, and Jason jotted it down in a small notebook.

"Where does Chris live?"

"You ain't gonna like this, man, but I've been straight with you. I don't know. He stays with his momma, and none of us was ever over there. Not ever."

"You're right. I don't like it. Not one bit."

Mumbo cringed, readying for the gunshot or kick to the bottom of the chair. Will's finger was tense on the controller, ready to loose another deluge of imaginary bullets into the wind. "But you know what? I believe you. One last question—anything else you can tell me about this fence?"

"Nah, man, nothing." Mumbo considered that before continuing. "Actually, man, I know one thing, but it won't do you any good."

"I'll be the judge of that. Tell me."

"Chris was never scared of anybody. But whoever that fence was? They scared the fuck out of him."

Jason nodded as if noting what Mumbo had told him, then took a dowel rod and a length of cord from his jacket pocket. Will watched him make a loop in the cord and run the dowel though it before he twisted it to make a bigger loop.

Mumbo's eyes got huge.

"Sorry, buddy, and thanks for the help," Jason said as he sat on the now violently struggling Mumbo's chest. Mumbo was screaming, thrashing about spastically, but Jason got the noose over his neck, and Jason began twisting the dowel, tightening the noose.

Will kept firing the gun on the TV as Mumbo died, even when he was through screaming. A coldness was coming over Will. His son had died for no reason, no reason at all. Just gunned down like a dog by one of his awful friends, and that was that. *No, that's not good enough. I need to know why. I need a reason. I cannot just walk away from this without an answer.* Will considered Alison's words, the steel in her voice when she told him to find the men who did this. And he thought of that night, so many years before, when he'd first laid eyes upon his boy.

* * *

Will was drunk, returning that summer night from a bonfire held out in a Jaycee-sponsored park. The party, of course, had not been sponsored. There'd been a ton of good grass, lots of blow, booze, and chicks who were down to party. His brother, Isaac, had even been there, and Isaac almost never went to shit like that, not since he'd turned twenty-one.

Walking home, Will felt so young and unstoppable that it was almost miraculous. At first, after Patty disappeared, things had been really shitty, but with the number of available girls in the world, it was hard to imagine why he'd even been upset in the first place. She was cool, but she was gone, and truth told, he wasn't even sure why his mind kept going back to her.

Patty had been cool for a while. Always there when he wanted her to be and always gone when he wanted her gone. It was enough to almost miss her, but then she'd gotten clingy after Jason and a few of the other guys had been sent up for breaking into that house. People had said some nasty shit about Jason after that had happened, like maybe he'd made some girl who was there blow him when she was supposed to be gone, but Will didn't think Jason had it in him. Besides, they were still only in county, with the real trials yet to even get going. Still, the kind of trouble they were in was sobering—or would've been, to someone less committed to the idea of getting fucked up every night. Even for a young drunk like him, it had been enough to convince him to maybe slow down a little. After all, he was supposed to have been with them that night.

Smash-and-grabs had been the thing that year. Break in and take anything not nailed down. They'd make off with a grand or more in televisions, stereos, jewelry, sometimes even other stuff, like guns. There was never much money in it, though. The pawnbrokers they dealt with had to ship the stuff out of the county, sometimes even out of the state, just to sell it without the law coming down.

That night had been different, though. When he'd gotten the call from Jason about the job a few days before, robbing a house while the family was on vacation, Will had been all about it. It wasn't until later, after the rest of them had gotten busted after a neighbor saw them, that Will questioned why he hadn't been there. Not feeling like it that night wasn't a good enough reason, but it was all he had. Still, there needed to be more. No one just got lucky like that, did they? Or was that the way the adult world really worked—a random succession of either good or bad breaks that could end with you doing life in Jackson or becoming the biggest rock star on the planet? Still, that had been the difference. He'd stayed home with Patty and watched comedies on the VCR—*Police Academy* and one of the *Vacation* flicks—but he didn't even have a good reason for it. He just knew that he didn't want to go.

He was on the stoop of his house when he first heard the crying. It sounded like a baby was wailing in his house. Not possible, though. They had no relatives with infants, and it was almost four in the morning, so somebody just stopping by was an impossible notion.

Opening the door quietly, Will couldn't help but notice that the crying was only getting louder. He pulled the door closed behind him, letting it ease into the frame, and walked into their family room. It wouldn't have been normal for his parents to leave the television on, but there was a first time for everything. Walking into the room, Will was stopped dead in his tracks.

His mother was sitting on a the couch across the room from the television holding an infant in her arms, trying—it looked like to Will, anyway—to calm it down. She was having limited success.

"Mom," Will slurred, "what the hell is going on?"

She patted the space next to her on the sofa, and Will sat, bidden by his mother in that way that is nearly impossible to resist.

"This," she said after Will had sat, "is Alex. He's your son." The baby had started to coo when Will sat, forgotten tears running down his impossibly tiny cheeks.

"My son? Who said that?"

"Patty did, that girl you used to date. She said that he was either yours or another boy's that she used to go around with—Jason, I think. She said that the other boy was in a lot of trouble and that her son needed a father."

"What did Dad say?"

"Your father has to work in the morning, as you know, and is sleeping with earplugs in. He does not know about Jason, and he is never going to. No one needs to know about that except for you and me. This is your son, and you're going to raise him right, like I raised you."

"I mean about me having a kid—what did he say?"

"Your father was taken aback, as was I, but he'll come around, just like I did. He may pull you aside and have a little talk, but I put my foot down. I said, 'This boy is a Daniels, your first grandson, and you may never get another one.' He knows that I mean it, too. We are going to raise this boy together, until you get your head straight and get a place for the two of you to live."

Will found himself staring at the baby, unsure of what to say. The boy definitely favored Patty, and they'd certainly had enough unprotected sex that it was possible, but what about the other stuff his mom had said? What if the boy wasn't his? What kind of life was that, raising another man's child while the other guy just got to go off and do whatever he wanted? That considered, Jason was probably going to prison; it was a foregone conclusion to most in their circle of friends.

"Mom, when did Patty say she was coming back?"

"Will," his mother said slowly, "Patty isn't coming back. This boy is only going to have a decent life if we can give him one. You might not feel like his father yet, but you will. Give it time. Give him time. He's your son, my grandson. He's a Daniels."

\* \* \*

Isaac was still standing in the doorway when Jason tapped Will on the shoulder. "You can stop shooting now." Will took his finger off the controller's trigger, then set down the controller. Jason gave him a look, so he stuck the thing in his jacket pocket before reholstering the Sig.

The three walked to the car in a group, and when Isaac began to choke on a mouthful of vomit, Jason took the keys from his hand and threw him headfirst behind the wheel.

**"W**hy in the fuck did you make me puke in my car?" Isaac screamed at Jason, vomit dripping from his mouth and covering his lap and the steering wheel.

Jason looked at Isaac from the passenger seat, smiled, and then slapped him, hard enough to spray the puke from his lips across the windshield. Will, sitting in the backseat now, thought for sure it was all going to unravel now. He had just watched a man be tortured and then strangled to death, and not only had he stood by and watched, but some small and very cruel part of him had enjoyed it. Hadn't Mumbo been there with Alex? He had, and if they were really friends, he would have killed Chris for shooting Alex, and none of this would have had to happen.

"You feel better now?" Jason asked Isaac, and Will was shocked to see his older brother nodding.

"You slapped me because we just killed a guy, and the cops would have probably tested my puke for DNA."

"Exactly. Now, roll down the windows, and drive to a gas station. I'll tell you when to turn."

"It's freezing back here with the windows down!" Will yelled, and Jason called back, "Can you still smell the puke?"

Realizing that he couldn't, or at least not as much, Will kept his mouth shut for the rest of the ride. Two minutes later, and one flashing red light, they pulled into a Marathon station.

"You guys stay put. I'm going to get some towels so we can get most of the sick off of you, and then you can go in the bathroom and wash up." Jason left the car, and the two brothers watched him walk inside to talk to the cashier.

"Are you OK, dude?" Will said it in a way that he thought might not be too offensive, but he could tell by Isaac's tone that he had failed.

"No. No, I'm not OK. I'm covered in puke, I feel like I've got a loose tooth from where he slapped me, and we could be charged with torturing and murdering that man. Not to mention we're about to go do the same thing again."

"I think we have to. If you ask Jason, he'll say the same thing. Right now, we've got the element of surprise. The cops aren't looking for us, and neither are the bad guys. I have a feeling that everything will stop after we find this Chris guy."

Will shut his mouth. They could see Jason returning to the car with a fistful of paper towels, a bathroom key attached to a hubcap by a chain, and a lit cigarette hanging from his lip. Isaac got out, and Jason handed him the towels, then went around to the passenger side and stood next to the car, smoking.

Most of the puke scraped off of Isaac and the dashboard, Jason handed him the key and pointed to the bathroom. "Over there." Jason and Will watched Isaac leave, and Jason said, "Will, get out."

Will did and stood beside him. Jason gave him a look, and Will said, "What?"

"Was it as bad as you thought?"

"No. Yes—I don't know. It was terrible, but even though he was kind of a funny guy, Mumbo shot up a bank for no reason other than that he was asked to do so. That's some seriously sociopathic shit."

"Yeah, it takes a certain type of individual to do something like that. Most of the guys I've known, even the really bad ones, wouldn't have done that unless they absolutely had to, and it never would have been part of the rules going in. To be frank, it's a really stupid plan and doesn't make any sense. Makes me excited to talk to Chris and Rob."

"What if they're not together? Mumbo said that no one knows where Chris lives."

"No matter what you're doing, there is always a solution to a problem, even if that solution turns out to be folding instead of going all-in. I have a feeling that Chris will be there. The question, and one I was worried about when we went to Mumbo's, is what your brother is going to do if we actually need his help. We got the drop on Mumbo pretty easily, but if we don't get the drop on these next two idiots, he could be a serious liability. I thought one of you might freeze, but Isaac was worse than frozen. He was trying to wish his way out of that room, and that's a dangerous thing to be doing. I don't need to remind you that this is all very serious, do I?"

"No, of course not."

Jason dropped the cigarette to the ground and crushed it with a boot. "Your brother will be back soon, and when he is, I want to go to Rob's place. We're right in the neighborhood, and if he hasn't already called Mumbo, he will soon, guaranteed. And he'll wonder when he doesn't get an answer. Is Isaac going to be able to do this or not?"

"Yes. I think so."

"You better hope so. We don't need him, but if he comes in, he needs to know that he needs to be there one hundred percent, no questions about it. Getting the drop on Mumbo means nothing now; we've got to do it all over again."

They saw Isaac returning from the bathroom, holding the hubcap and key in his hands like some bizarre trophy. Will could see in the lights from the gas station that his brother's shirt was stained, but otherwise, what remained of the puke had been washed away. Jason and Will piled in the car, Will back in the front seat. Isaac got behind the wheel, stuck his key in the ignition, and Jason said, "Forgetting something?"

"Oh shit, the key." The hupcap and key were sitting right there in his lap. Isaac began opening his door, and Jason said, "No, give it to me. Better they only see one of us." He took it from Isaac, left the car, and sauntered back to the gas station.

"Are we going to the next house?" Isaac asked, and Will said, "Yes. Can you handle that?"

"Yeah. I can. The first time was just bad. This will be easier, right?"

"I wouldn't count on it."

\* \* \*

It took them a while to get to Rob's house, but when they did, it looked like they'd just circled the block. This street and Mumbo's were clones of one another, and Will wondered how big these eerily similar suburbs were. The address they'd had for Rob matched the one on a gray house that needed paint, and Isaac parked a few houses away. There were two cars in the driveway, and the street was littered with vehicles, many more than what they'd seen at Mumbo's.

"No freezing up this time," said Jason. "None of that shit. You busted your cherry, and this time needs to go better. There are either a lot of people sharing houses here, or someone is having a party. Now, I'm assuming it's not Rob, because Mumbo would have been here instead of playing video games, but it is a possibility. Are you guys ready?"

Will let the air collapse from his lungs and said, "Yes."

Isaac just nodded. It must have looked more impressive in the front than it did to Will, because Jason returned the nod with one of his own.

"Just like last time," said Jason. "I'll go first. You guys come in right after me. Remember, just like you saw me do to Mumbo, it's all about the first fifteen seconds. If you shatter their confidence, they'll let you do just about anything." With that, they left the car.

Just as he had the last time, though without even bothering to look at what Jason was doing, Will had his pistol out and pressed to his side.

There were fewer house lights on than when they'd gone into Mumbo's, but the street felt more alive. Will followed Jason onto the porch. It had a waist-high wall and was covered in cigarette butts and empty beer bottles and cans. Will could feel Isaac behind him, and the sound of loud rap music was coming from the house. As Jason kicked the door in, Will could hear a girl laughing.

**W**alking in behind Jason, Will saw a white man, naked from the waist down, sitting on a filthy sofa. In his lap was the head of a girl in her late teens or early twenties giving him a blow job. Jason walked quickly across the room toward them with his pistol up, Will doing the same thing, and neither of them had been noticed yet. The rap was much louder than it had been outside, booming, and there was a loud thumping noise coming from upstairs. More music. Finally, when they were but a few yards from him, the man opened his eyes and jumped slightly.

The girl working in his lap gagged, lifted her head up, and said to him, "What the fuck?" She turned to look at them, eyes widening, and as Jason raised his finger to his mouth to say, *Shhh*, the girl began to scream.

The man jumped off the couch, throwing the girl away from him like a doll as he dove to the floor toward a pair of jeans lying next to the couch. Jason and Will fired at the same time, one of their bullets hitting him in the back, the other removing a piece of thigh. The girl was still screaming, and Jason walked to her and hit her on the top of the head with his pistol, collapsing her to the floor instantly. Another gun went off, and both Will and Jason jumped, Will's eyes darting around the room, finally noticing the hole in the side of the man on the floor's head.

"He was still going for his gun," explained Isaac. "I had to."

"You did good," Jason said, then grabbed the dead man by the hair and began rifling through his jeans, taking a cell phone from one of the pockets and stuffing it into his own pocket. "Find something and tie her up—gag her too. Do a good job, but do it fast. If you get the chance, try and find the shell casings. Will, come with me." Walking quickly, pistol held aloft, Jason left the room. Sparing his brother a look, Will turned, his Sig at the ready, and followed Jason into a black hallway.

The thumping noise from upstairs, audible before, even with the music, had stopped.

They made their way swiftly from the quasi foyer/living room and walked into a kitchen, the only light source coming from a single bulb hanging from a string. There were three doors in the kitchen, one of them clearly leading to the backyard. Jason opened one of the others, stuck his gun into the blackness, and over his shoulder, Will could see descending stairs. Jason left the first door open and slowly began to open the second. The stairs in that one went up, and there was a single door at the top of the steps.

Jason took the phone that he'd stolen from the dead man's pants out of his pocket and began to do something with it— Will couldn't tell exactly what—and then he put it to his ear and began to ascend the stairs. When the sound of a ringing phone came to them, barely audible over the thumping bass and spoken bravado, Jason and Will ran up the stairs, Jason kicking the door open, both of their guns up and ready.

The timing couldn't have been more perfect. There was a skinny white kid in the room holding a large stainless-steel revolver, but he was pointing it at the floor, distracted by that god of the modern era, his ringing cell phone. On the bed behind him were two girls, one white and one black. All three of them were naked. Just loud enough to be heard over the rap, and with both of their guns trained on the kid—it was hard to see him as any-thing but a kid—Jason said, "Drop the gun, or you're dead. Do it now." There was a moment of hesitation, and the kid dropped the gun to the floor.

"Girls, off the bed," Jason said, training his gun at the black girl as Will kept his own slightly shaky barrel on the kid. "You first," Jason commanded, pistol still on the black girl. "Go downstairs, and do it slowly. My partner down there has an itchy trigger finger. You'll want to ask him if you can come in."

The girl slid off of the bed and bent slowly to retrieve an article of clothing from the floor. She was beautiful.

"Did I tell you to get your shit? Get your ass down there."

The girl just shrugged, and Jason's pistol followed her until she was down the stairs and gone.

The kid smiled thinly at Will as the girl left, looking at his gun, then at Will, as though trying to show that he hadn't lost all control of the situation.

Jason pointed his pistol at the blonde white girl on the bed. She looked furious. "You look like you want to do something very stupid," Jason said to her. "And if you try and do that stupid thing, I will kill you. I know that you might think I'm bluffing, that my partner and I won't shoot you, but we will. We will end your little meaningless life and then go out for pancakes and never give you another thought."

The girl, looking even angrier now, slid slowly off the bed. Will kept his eyes on the kid, who was making it obvious that he was going to try for the gun at his feet, the gun that he had very likely used to kill Alex. Will's resolve, and grip on the pistol, went back to iron, how he'd been before Mumbo. If the kid could see the difference, he wasn't showing it.

"Get your ass downstairs," said Jason to the angry girl, "and if my partner isn't ready for you, sit on the fucking couch so he doesn't have to kill anyone else tonight."

The kid just kept smiling. When the girl was gone, Jason walked to the kid's revolver, picked it up, and handed it to Will, both of their guns back on the kid. Will felt numb with the gun in his hand, the gun that had very likely killed his son. He wanted to kill Chris and leave, but that wasn't enough, not yet. Not even close.

* * *

"Chris," Jason said, the kid's smile crumbling at the sound of his name, "we need to talk, buddy. Rob is dead downstairs, and I had to kill Mumbo just to find you guys.

"Now, first things first," Jason went on, "our man downstairs is going to hustle your ladies into the basement, and then we're going to go for a little ride, make sure the law isn't coming after those gunshots. Just my two buddies, me, and of course, you, asshole."

Chris spit in Jason's face. Jason shook his head and smashed Chris across the face with his pistol, likely breaking his nose and dropping him to the floor of the room.

"Will, go make sure your brother is having fun, and help him get those bitches down to the basement. I need to tie up this motherfucker's wrists."

Will did as he was told, quite sure that Jason could manage Chris easily enough, and headed down the steps. Crossing first through the kitchen and then emerging into the living room, Will thought the situation felt surreal, like something in one of his books. Isaac had the three girls on the couch, though the first one, the one Will had hit on the head, was still unconscious and sitting in a pile of piss, with her gag lying on her breasts. Rob was where Will had last seen him and was still quite dead.

"We need to get the girls in the basement," Will said. "You two that are still mobile, get your asses moving. Find something to tie them to, all right?"

"Sure thing," said Isaac, and as he spoke, Will found himself hoping, not for the first time, that neither he nor his brother would slip up and use each other's names. "Get up. Get your butts in gear."

The girls obliged, first standing with bound wrists and gagged mouths, then walking silently, with Isaac following them. Will regarded the unconscious one, finally settling on holstering his pistol in his over-the-shoulder rig and then hoisting the girl up. For someone who looked like she subsisted on a diet of cocaine and semen, she was surprisingly heavy. Will managed her weight as best he was able. It had been a long time since he'd lifted anyone, even Alison, and he could feel his back screaming at him.

Will could see Isaac at the bottom of the steps, binding the girls' wrists together around a pole, the girls back-to-back against it. Struggling against his girl's weight, each step was a small hell. Will could hear Chris and Jason arguing as they came down the steps from the room upstairs, and that was just enough to distract him from the fact that the girl he'd thought was unconscious had come to life.

She had his Sig out of its holster before Will even had the chance to react. "Put me down, motherfucker," the girl said, screeching, "before I fucking shoot you!" Will was moving to oblige her, he could feel the barrel pushing into his stomach, but at the last minute, he changed his mind, giving her a twist and bucking her off of his shoulder, then driving her to the stairs with his hands.

She landed on her right shoulder on a step—her collarbone or something in her shoulder crunching and the pistol flying from her hands—and then her neck collided with the next step down, making a sound that reminded Will of separating chicken bones. The girl slid down the rest of the steps, clearly dead, her neck bent at an impossible angle. The girls tied to the pole watched her slide to the bottom, then began violently thrashing against their restraints and attempting to scream through their gags. Isaac walked to the steps, picked up Will's pistol off the floor next to the dead girl, pulled a cord attached to a light, and the brothers left the girls to struggle in the darkness.

Jason was waiting for them at the top of the stairs. Chris was still grinning like an idiot, but there was some new damage to his face, and he'd also acquired a limp. His nose was still bleeding too, but just looking at his stupid smile made Will want to smack him, even with his injuries, and want to do much worse things as well. *This man killed my son, and the gun he did it with is in my pocket.* As hard as it was not to just shoot Chris and leave, that would have been the end of it, and the real reason for Alex's death would always be a mystery.

"Get your ass moving," Jason said to Chris. "C'mon, let's get in the car, go for a little ride. And remember what I said, play nice."

Will and Isaac followed Jason and Chris outside. There were no sirens, at least not yet, and Will was happy for that small bit of luck. Jason had his jacket off and folded over his arm, presumably to conceal a gun, because the hand under the jacket was pushed into Chris's back. Isaac unlocked the car and got in, Chris and Jason got into the back, and Will sat up front again. "Drive," said Jason, "ten minutes anywhere, and then drive us right back here."

\* \* \*

Isaac drove the Camry off Chris's street, took another turn, and was back onto Ivanrest, a much busier street, bordered by a mix of residences and businesses.

The adrenaline from being in the house was starting to wear off, and Will's realization that he had shot a man was starting to weigh on him. The girl was different somehow, not his fault. Even if he had bounced her off the steps, she had been ready to shoot him, and with her wrists bound together as they were, the bullet could have gone anywhere. *All she had to do was let me get her downstairs,* thought Will, though he had not yet let his mind decide what Jason's plan for the fate of the girls might be. After all, the girls had seen their faces.

"This is a waste of time, motherfuckers," said Chris, no swagger in his voice, just ice. "I'm not going to give you shit, and that money, other than the few g's that idiot Mumbo just had to have, is long gone. The real check is yet to come, so you boys missed motherfuckin' payday by a hot minute."

"You think this is about the money you stole?" Will said from the front seat, anger unsuppressed in his voice. "This is about my son, Alex."

"Oh shit," said Chris, all bravado gone, finally. "You ain't after money at all, is you?"

"Well," said Jason, "some of us wouldn't mind finding your score, but this is more about getting information, and if you don't have any, this is going to be a long night, with no morning to follow it."

"Well, shit, you put it like that, just ask away. I'll tell you everything I know. Hey, my man, front seat. Alex was a friend of mine. He was a cold motherfucker, a good dude too. But you said you his father, no offense, but Alex always said his dad was just some drunk-ass writer. No offense. Mumbo tell you I shot him?"

"Yes," said Will.

"See, now that's the problem these days," opined Chris. "Mumbo was about to die either way, and I bet he gave me up like vegetables on his plate. You at least have to hurt him?"

"I hurt him very much," said Jason. "He forced me to."

"Hey, I'm not judging that. Sometimes that's how it has to be. Shit, truth of it is I'm glad you had to put the screws to him a little bit. Dude was always a little soft."

"Why did you shoot up the bank?" Jason asked. "It made no sense to do that."

"Shit, that's exactly what I said. Alex shot that dude, and then Mumbo just went off. Shit happens. But the thing is, none of that happened because of money. Everything there was a smoke screen. You going to want to be careful we go any further on that shit, though. Even by just coming after me, you guys have thrown your hat into some nasty shit, and seeing as how I'm expecting to hear from my man soon, I have a bad feeling some of this shit might get stuck to your shoes too.

"Now, before you come back and tell me that you're not worried about some punk motherfucker like me, you need to know that just because you got the drop on Mumbo, which was probably just luck, and the drop on me, which was just damn good luck, doesn't mean you guys got a chance with the big man. He'll chew you up and spit out a bunch of crushed-up bones."

Jason chuckled. "It wasn't luck that let us get the jump on you. It was plain old cockiness on your part and nothing else. You should have been sitting with your friend, armed and waiting for something like this to happen, and you should have been with Mumbo." To Isaac, he said, "This is far enough. Drive back to the house."

Chris piped up. "Man, see that's exactly what I'm talking about. We've been sitting tight as two nuts in a sac, waiting for some shit just like this to happen."

"Hey, check it out," said Isaac. "It's all ice-age snow, and now it's raining. That's crazy."

"Yeah, it's nuts, crazy," said Jason. "Chris, I want to know who this guy is and what exactly you were really doing at that bank. If it wasn't for money, then why did you pick that spot, and why did you shoot Alex if he was such a good friend? I'm really having a hard time with some of it, mostly because it all sounds like total bullshit."

"It happened like this."

* * *

"My boys and I got to eat, right? So when a job comes along, and it sounds like something some of my boys and I can do without causing us too much shit, we do it.

"This job, the bank one, wasn't something I was initially very high on. It sounded like a high-risk thing, and everybody knows that all that bank money is marked and recorded by the FBI, specifically to keep people like me from doing the dirty on 'em, coming in strapped and just taking that shit. Anyways, my man, Jefe, he says that this job isn't like that, and I'm not supposed to share that shit with anybody, especially not the guys doing the job with me. I remember asking him why, and he said he would try and set up a meeting with me and the dude who wanted the shit done, so I said cool.

"Anyways, Jefe called me back the same day, just later that night. I had just smoked out, and I was feeling good about shit, especially if we could get the job. I knew that Mumbo was getting hard up, and it had been a little while since we had a score that wasn't just nickel-and-dime bullshit. So when my phone rang and I saw it was Jefe, I was like, 'Cool,' you know? So I answered the phone, and Jefe said that he had talked to his dude, and we could meet. I asked him when he thought that might be, and he asked if I was at Rob's or Mumbo and Alex's house. I don't know how he knew I wasn't at Mom's—maybe he could tell I was high. Mom doesn't play that shit for a minute, but she'll take money I make off of doing stuff a lot worse than just selling dope. Sort of fucked up, when you think about it.

"I told him I was at Mumbo and Alex's, and he said that a car would be there to pick me up in an hour. I was like, 'Oh shit, a car?' It all seemed fancy as hell to me. I've worked with and for a lot of motherfuckers, but nobody ever just says, 'I'll send a car for you.' That's like getting off a plane and seeing a nigga in a suit holding a sign with your name on it, big-time shit, you know? I told Mumbo and Alex that some guy was sending a car over so that I could talk to him about a job. Their eyes got all big like I expected, big-time shit, you know? I just acted like it was no big deal, but I figured if they had money to come get me in a car, they might have real money, make this a real score, not just a job to tide me over for a month or two. Ask any cop, mistakes come in volume in crime, usually not just in one job, unless you're a fucking idiot, and that was making me nervy. We were pulling all these little jobs just to get right, when fewer bigger jobs were what we needed.

"So I'm looking out the window and this car pulls up, black, all black windows, no logos anywhere on it. I mean, I'm sure it was just a regular car with perks, boosted engine, bulletproof glass, maybe solid rubber tires, but that thing was fucking awesome. My crew, guys my age, we all want like a bright-orange Camaro on dubs, you know? Something flashy, make girls want to get a ride, make other dudes want what you got. This was gangster, but like a grown-up gangster. It was bad as a motherfucker.

"I got off that couch, said later to Mumbo and Alex, and walked outside. I had such a good feeling about it I didn't even bring a heater, and I always stay strapped.

"When I got outside, a dude was standing next to the car, wearing a suit and shit, and he opened the door for me. I got in the backseat, and there was a dude sitting there with weird makeup on his face. Looked like he'd passed out and somebody had hit him up with a Sharpie. He hands me a black bag and says real slowly in fucked-up English, 'Put on your head.' I wanted to say something, but that motherfucker, Magic Marker face or not, was seriously kind of tripping me out, so I just put the bag on my head like he told me to.

"We drove for a while. I don't know how long. I should have kept track by counting, I guess, but it's not like it really mattered. I was going somewhere, and I was going to do whatever the dude I was supposed to meet said to do. I didn't feel like a big badass anymore. I was scared, and something about that dude's marker face was sticking in my head sideways, like I knew what it was but couldn't quite get my brain wrapped around it.

"Finally, the car stopped. I heard the door open, and somebody yanked me out of the car and pulled me to my feet.

"I still had the hood on, but it was nice to be out of the car. The dude in back with me didn't smell the best. I didn't notice it at first, but the longer I was back there, the smell came through the hood, and the only thing I can think to compare that shit to is death. That dude smelled like a corpse, that's just all there is to it.

"So I'm out of the car and walking with a hand not on my back but sort of hovering over it. I hear a door open, and it's loud as fuck. At that point, I was trying to take in anything I could, and that was definitely a steel door, a heavy one, in a steel doorframe. I could feel the temperature change, so I knew I was inside. Plus, I could tell I was walking on indoor cement now—there was no slush or snow. Then they took the hood off of me.

"The first thing I saw was a fucking machine gun; it was pointed at my face, a couple of inches away, tops. The guy holding it was wearing a bandanna over his face and had his hood pulled up, but it looked like he had some of that marker shit on his face too. I just stared right down that barrel while some other dude frisked me. When he was done, he said something in Spanish, and the dude with the machine gun lowered it so that it was pointed at my chest. Sort of an improvement, but not really, you know?

"The guy with a gun is staring me down and finally starts nodding his head, and then he says, 'Sigueme,' and starts walking away from me. The dude who was frisking me starts pushing a gun into my back, and I was like, 'OK, cool, follow Machine Gun Guy.'

"He walks through another steel door and gestures for me to come on in. I do, and the guy who was behind me stays in the first room, so it's just me and the other dude. He motions at a chair. It had some dried blood on it, but I tell myself not to worry; they were going to way too much trouble just to kill me. I sit down, and Machine Gun Guy stands by a door opposite of the one we came into the room through, the gun across his chest. That door opens, and Machine Gun Guy leaves, and I was alone.

"A few minutes later, another dude comes in. He's got a suit on, but there are tattoos all over his face; he almost looks like he has a mask on. There's a big *M* over half of it and a big *S* over the other half. He had the cartilage cut off of his ears, and there was a scar across his throat, like somebody had almost killed this fucker, but he lived somehow. He looks at me and says in perfect English, 'How are you doing, Chris?'

"'I'm doing fine,' I said. 'What can I help you with, Mr.—'

"'My name does not matter. Nothing about this matters except for what I'm about to tell you. If you can do this job, I will make you rich. If you fail, you will die. If you say no today, my man will come back in here and kill you. There will be nothing you can do about it. Are we clear?'

"'Yes, sir.'

"'Good. I need a job done. On February eighteenth, I need you to rob Great Lakes Credit Union branch four twenty-one. I want it to look like a regular robbery. I want you to take money and say scary things. I want it to be clean, but if you need to kill people to get me what I want…the only other thing I care about, besides this looking like a regular robbery that got nasty, is that you open safety deposit box number eleven thirty-eight and take its contents. No one is to know about this, aside from you. The contents of that box are going to be there on that day alone, and I need what's in that box.

"'If one of your partners finds out that you have taken something from that box, you must kill him. If all of your partners find that you took from this box, you must kill all of them. I do not care if they do not know what was in that box, but if they so much as mention it, they must die. If you think there is a possibility that they know about it, they have to die. There is no negotiating this. Perhaps you kill them just to make sure I think you take care of business? That's fine with me. But, Chris, if I find out that one of them knows, and you do not kill them, you die a bad way. You don't want that. I don't want that. I just want what's in that box, and I want that to be between you and me. No one from my crew knows, just you and just me.

"'If you see what's in the box, you put that thought out of your mind—you make it all the way gone. You see it if you have to, like if it is not packaged, but then you forget you ever see it. Understand?'

"'If you think I saw what was in that box,' I said, 'then I die a bad way.'

"'Yes, Chris,' the dude said, and he looked sad when he said it, like he knew he was putting me in a bad spot. I couldn't say no, because then I died right away. I couldn't tell anybody on my crew the truth. I mean, no one would do a job like that, no matter how much money it was worth. I just had to act like I set up a bunch of stuff myself, based on a tip. I had a tip, all right, and it was going to get us all killed, I just knew it.'"

\* \* \*

They'd been back at the house in Isaac's parked Camry for about five minutes as Chris finished the story. Will had a hard time believing it, but it all made sense.

The wind was howling and battering rain at them while they sat in the car. Will could feel the gun in his jacket, the one the girl had tried to take away, and realized just how tired he was, like someone had been slowly scraping the life from him and was just now letting him know what they'd been up to.

"So you hooked up with MS-Thirteen," said Jason. "You should have just said no and let them kill you."

"I know," said Chris, "but it's too late for that."

"C'mon, let's get back in the house. Law ain't coming." Jason said it with malice, but Will could hear something else in his voice, and Will was pretty sure what he was hearing was fear. *If Jason is scared, then what the fuck am I supposed to be doing, running away?* Will tried to ignore the thought, push it away like it had never happened. He got out of the car, following Isaac, Jason, and Chris across the street.

The rain was falling like mad now, snow disappearing from the lawns like a magic trick. Lightning crashing, thunder rumbling, like the weather could somehow understand the fix they were in.

"Jason, what's MS-Thirteen?" Isaac asked as they walked.

Jason, still walking forward, replied, "MS-Thirteen started in El Salvador. They're the kind of gang that other gangs are scared of. They're brutal and very efficient. They favor tattooed faces and machetes, and they're supposed to be scared of nothing. I read once about how they even had their own language so they could communicate secretly in prison. Fuckhead here got lucky too. Worst he'll see from us is something quiet. Of course, he could get lucky, keep saying what I want to hear. Those dudes? They'll cut his dick off and feed it to him, pull his tongue through his throat, wrap him in tires, coat him in gas, and let him burn. I forgot that part—they're famously creative. Open the door."

Chris obliged him, opening the door and walking into the house, but not rushing, knowing that to try and get away from Jason would just mean a bullet in the back.

"So what now?" Will asked.

"Well, we're going to see to your man here, and then I'm going to ice the girls in the basement. After that, we're going to leave and hope that we can forget any of this ever happened."

"Hey," said Will, "somebody turned off the music."

Jason threw Chris, hard. The kid bounced over a coffee table, landing face-first in the piss that was partially soaked into the couch. "Time to go, guys," said Jason. "Right now, go."

It was too late.

The house must have been filled with bangers, and they filed into the living room quickly. The men wore hoods and bandannas across their faces. The most minimally armed of them had pistols; the rest had AK-47 or AR-15 semiautomatic rifles. Between the hoods and bandannas, their tattoos were visible.

Jason dropped his gun, and Isaac followed suit. Will was last, slowly laying the Sig on the floor and then placing the revolver that Chris had given to Jason next to it. Two of the men came over and collected their pistols, and a third began to frisk them. He took a small automatic from Jason's right ankle and a revolver from his lower back. Will could feel the man grinning at them through his bandanna, tattoos savaged into the skin above his eyes, while another took their phones and everything else that was in their pockets.

"You got something for my friend?" said one of the men in the group. He was holding one of the short-barreled AR-15s and clearly talking to Chris.

"Yeah," said Chris, "it's upstairs. You want me to go get it?"

"*Si*." The man barked something else in Spanish, and two of the other men walked to Chris. The three of them left the room. Will could hear their feet as they went up the stairs. No one said anything while Chris was gone. Will, Jason, and Isaac just stared at the feet of the men who were now in control of the situation.

Noise on the stairs again snapped Will's head back up, and Chris and the other two men came sauntering back into the room. Chris had a backpack slung over one shoulder, and the swagger that had turned to fear was back. Chris had lucked out; he was winning. It made Will sick. Not because he was probably going to die soon, but that he'd had the chance—thousands of chances, really—to kill Chris and just walk away. He hadn't, though. He'd been so sure that he needed to get to the bottom of everything, but there was no bottom. A man with lots of power was going to see to their ends. Will would never get to see Alison again, never get to enjoy the life that he had left and had always taken for granted.

As they were walked out of the house into a pair of waiting black vans, Will wanted to run so they'd be forced to shoot him in the streets. Getting into the van, he wasn't sure what was worse: not having the balls to run or that they weren't even bothering to cover their heads with hoods, like Chris had said they'd done to him. Will sat with a banger on either side of him, behind him Isaac was similarly surrounded, and in the row in front of him, Will could see that Jason was as well. When Chris got into the van and sat two rows in front of him, Will could hear him cracking jokes to himself, the idiot not yet realizing that no hood for him this time meant that the real joke was on him too.

Lightning flashed again, and the wind buffeted the still-stationary van, making it bobble right to left as the thunder crashed around them. *What an odd night for a thunderstorm*, Will thought. Storms in late February or early March weren't impossible, but they were not a common thing, not by a long shot. Hail came with the rain, pitter-pattering off of the van like shot rolling down a tin roof. No one else in the vehicle seemed to notice, so Will tried to ignore it as well. Still, it was odd. A near blizzard two days ago, a thunderstorm this late in winter, and now pea-sized hail, maybe even bigger than that. It was a fitting end to the night, a winter maelstrom still deciding what type of storm it wanted to be, snow or thunder, ice, or lightning.

The driver of their van was cursing in Spanish. Will couldn't understand the words, but he was clearly not very happy. The weather had not gotten any better since they'd left the southwest side, the rain and hail mixed with occasional blasts of snow. A weatherman would have called it "wintry mix"—cold and warm fronts clashing to create conditions that could be politely described as difficult to drive in. One of the men next to Will was ignoring it, playing a game on his phone, but the other, a boy younger than Alex at the time of his death, looked terrified. Will didn't blame him.

The van was rocking so much that Will felt as though he were on a ship. The windows around them were fouled by weather; the rain made the snow stick to the van, and then more rain would glaze it into a thick crust. Only the front windshield remained clean, and that was only because the wipers were working at a frenetic pace. Will couldn't see the speedometer well enough to read it from where he sat, but he would have guessed their speed at no more than thirty miles per hour. There were almost no other cars on the road for them to have to worry about, but Will thought he understood the fear in some of the men and in the eyes of the driver.

The package Chris had secured obviously had some sort of significance beyond what some random little trinket in a bag could have supplied. The crew of gangbangers that had met them at the house hadn't been sent to stop them; they were still a wildcard. The show of force was a coincidence, likely intended for the intimidation and probable deaths of Mumbo and Rob. The gangsters were likely as shocked to see them back at the house as they had been to see the gangsters there.

An especially strong gust of wind threatened to spill the van, but the vehicle righted itself, the driver spitting a song of foreign obscenities as the bulky vehicle regained its footing.

*They're going to take us to wherever they took Chris, to a place with bloody chairs and grinning men who smell like death,* thought Will. Where could that be? Had they been headed south on 131, the highway that splices through the middle of Grand Rapids, he would have assumed they were heading to a farm or slaughterhouse. Since it would have been faster to take Ivanrest to the northwest side, especially in this weather, Will decided they were being brought north of Alpine. There were a number of nondescript warehouses out there, the *Grand Rapids Press* had one of its own among the anonymous others. It would be a perfect place—outside the city, but close enough to be there in ten minutes if need be. Passing through the lights adorning the tall buildings of Grand Rapids, Will felt miserable that this was the last time he was going to see them.

How long would Alison wait to remarry? Hopefully not long. She deserved to be happy. Would his death be anonymous, or would they let his body be found? Will assumed the former was far more likely; why give the police anything to work with? There was nothing holding back his tears and his fear beyond a dignity he was only now discovering in himself, a determination to die with dignity, or at least as much dignity as he was capable of if the MS-13 leader decided that he needed to die a bad death.

The wind was really howling now that they'd left the city, moving their van back and forth. Will could no longer see the taillights of the other van traveling in front of them. Their driver was doing a pretty good job, considering. They passed by Alpine, its normally bright retail lights nearly smothered by the weather, the parking lots that Will could see empty and the almost always clogged traffic nonexistent.

The weather was some of the worst Will had ever seen, but as they passed the first exit ramp past Alpine, it somehow got worse. The younger, nervous man sitting next to Will said, "Shit," in a thick Latin accent. Just then, through the window, Will could barely make out what looked like a giant tearing off the top of a warehouse, just as a regular man would tear the top from a tin of sardines. The sound it made was horrible, an otherworldly screech. The van swerved, Will assumed to avoid something, and then Jason was smashing the bandanna-covered face of the man next to him with an elbow and shooting the man's carry piece into the front of the van. The noise from the gun was louder than anything Will had ever heard, and the men around him were covering their ears and shouting rather than attacking Jason. At that moment, as Jason was finding a way to free them, or at least himself, the world went upside down. The same hand of God that had been tearing the top from the building seemed to lift them as well, and then the van was airborne and spinning.

* * *

Will awoke confused, and then the fear came back to him. *We crashed.* He began trying to move as his eyes adjusted to the darkness and to the pile of unconscious and possibly dead men around him.

As worried as he was about his brother, his priority was to make sure he was going to be in a safe enough position to try to help Isaac and help himself. Will's body felt made of aches. He heard a voice begin swearing in Spanish, and then that voice was extinguished as another voice said, "Choke on that, motherfucker."

*Jason,* thought Will, trying to pull enough air into his lungs to call for what he was starting to think of as his old friend.

Will's eyes continued orienting themselves to the darkness, as well as to the odd shapes that the ruined van and even more ruined bodies were taking on. The gang members were everywhere. The scared kid who'd been sitting next to him had his brains leaking out of his ears and his nose. Already having a rather deplorable day, Will had no problem with rooting around for the kid's pistol, finding it tucked into the waist of his pants and taking it for himself. He slowly racked it to check the chamber. The gun was a Glock and had not been taken care of properly. It would have to work.

Will began to slide, pistol first, to the back of the van, which, he now finally realized, lay upside down. This helped him make some sense of the scene. The seat he had been in was fine above him, but the roof over it—now the floor under Will's knees—had been crumpled like an accordion, making the trip to attempt to find Isaac into a series of valleys and hills. One of the MS-13 members groaned when Will placed his hands on him, and Will responded by hitting the man in the throat with the butt of the pistol until he stopped complaining. The wind was blowing snow into the distressed van, and Will could hear Jason dealing with another one of the bangers in his own way, but he didn't care; he could see Isaac's shirt, and the shirt was covered in blood.

Next to Isaac, or at least what Will could see of him, one of the bangers was starting to stir. Will, sore or not, increased his pace, the pistol in front of him. Behind him, Will could hear a struggle. That, and hearing Jason say "son of a bitch" awoke something in him. Will turned, the pistol coming up naturally, somehow, and shot the banger holding Jason in the head, dropping him. Will had only fired a Glock a couple of times, and the weird part was how quiet the gun was, almost no noise in the van. *My ears*, Will thought, as he raced—well, crawled—back to Isaac and his bloody shirt.

Isaac was underneath one banger, plus half of another. Will could feel, if not hear, another gun go off near what had been the cab of the van, but chose to ignore it. He shoved the sawn-in-half MS-13 member off of his brother's prone body and was happy to see that Isaac was still intact, at least from the waist down. Someone behind Will, in the front of the van, began to scream, then stopped as a sputter of hail attacked the ruined vehicle. When the hail passed, the scream had become a gurgling noise. Will dragged the other man covering his brother from off of Isaac, then began scrabbling at his brother's wrist to try to feel for a pulse.

Isaac was alive. Twin bubbles of snot and spit were inflating and then deflating under his nostrils, and Will was sure he could hear him moaning.

The sound of thumping came from the front of the van, and craning his neck, Will could see Jason beating another one of the gangbangers to death with the butt of a pistol.

"Get your fucking brother, Will!" Jason was screaming at him, and Will, terrified that he was going to somehow damage Isaac further, began to crawl over the dying and dead while dragging Isaac by his feet. His brother wasn't stirring, which Will took as a bad sign, but tried to just ignore it. Something grabbed at his leg, and Will jumped, almost screamed.

"It's just me," said Jason. "Hold on tight."

The tugging on his leg grew stronger, and then first Will and then Isaac were out of the van and onto the highway. The wind was insane, but relief flooded Will. They were alive. He looked for the other van, but other than some tracks leading off the highway, it was gone. He gave Isaac a glance, knowing that a day of hauling his older brother around was just beginning, and then turned to Jason.

Jason was bleeding from a cut over his right eye but met Will's glance with a grin. He was holding an AK-47 that he must have taken from one of the dead bangers and tossed a short-barreled AR-15 to Will, a semiauto with some sort of sight on top. Will fiddled with the sight for a moment. Then, after pushing a button on the back of it, a small red dot surrounded by a red circle was visibly projected onto a clear, square piece of glass. Will took the safety off and lowered it.

Jason was moving Isaac to a sitting position, then picked him up over his shoulder. "We need to find your brother some shelter."

"Don't you think we should just get out of here?"

"Look over there," said Jason, pointing to the shoulder of the road. If there had been footprints, they were erased by the wind, but a distinct blood trail, likely only minutes old, was headed north. "Chris isn't in the van," said Jason, "and neither was his backpack. From what I remember, and counted, there's at least one of these fuckers missing as well, maybe two of them. I smell gas. Let's go."

Jason began moving down the highway, Isaac slung over his shoulder, the small AK in his free hand. Will was the rear guard, wondering to himself if anything could kill or even scare Jason.

* * *

The blood trail went up the next exit ramp, and they followed it through the wind, ice, rain, and snow, the storm becoming as much an adversary as the room full of armed and angry gangbangers had been. If Jason was having trouble with Isaac, he wasn't showing it, or at least wasn't mentioning it.

The blood trail was visible off the ramp and headed down on a street called Fruitridge. Just off the exit ramp, Will could see a gas station, its sign and pumps destroyed by the storm, as it became visible through the maelstrom.

Jason led them to the gas station, a battered Sunoco that had not only lost its pumps and sign, but also its windows and electricity. Setting Isaac down next to the door, Jason fiddled with the lock through the shattered glass and then opened it. Will grabbed his brother's shoulders, attempted to pick him up, and settled on dragging him into the gas station. He had no idea how Jason had carried him down the highway and up the ramp.

Stopping once they were inside the station, he found Jason across the room, looking around. "Over there," he said, pointing to a wooden door that looked like it still had some integrity left.

Jason opened the door to the windowless manager's office, and Will dragged Isaac inside, leaning him against a desk. Jason took a coat hanging off the back of the door and wrapped it around Isaac.

"Do you think he'll be OK in here?" Will asked. "He's totally out of it."

"Well," said Jason, "if the pumps were going to blow, they'd already be tits up. Looks like somebody had the good sense to hit the cutoff on the gas before they got the hell out of here. Hey, small miracles."

"I mean, just leaving him, though. Will he be all right?"

"I don't know, and neither do you. I do know that neither of us have a cell phone and that, even if we did, there would be no fucking reception out here in this storm." Jason picked up a wired phone receiver from the desk, held it to his ear for a second, and replaced it. "Landlines are down too, so either we sit here and hold your brother's hand while we wait for morning or we go after this asshole. To be entirely honest, I'm going either way. Those fucks were going to kill me, and that's not something that sits easy."

"All right, I'm in too. I'm going to get some water and food to put by him, in case he wakes up. Will you find something in here to write on and leave him a note?"

"You want me to put on some lipstick and kiss the note too?"

"No, I think the note and supplies will be enough." Will grinned despite himself. "I'll be right back, and I'm serious about the note."

Will walked into the store part of the gas station, grabbed two bottles of water from a cooler with blown-out glass doors, then also grabbed a can of Pringles and a couple packs of beef jerky.

When he came back into the office, he found Isaac lying on the floor with a note on his chest that said, *Back soon, stay here.* Will set the food and water next to his brother, then stood watching as Jason half-racked the bolt on the AR.

"They're both loaded," Jason said, "but we don't have any spare magazines, so if you have to shoot at someone, make sure it's worth doing. You see these?" He pointed fore and aft on the small carbine. "If that cute little dot sight gets fucked up, hit the buttons on the sides of those, and you'll be back in the game, assuming you're worth a shit with iron sights."

"I'm not."

"Well," said Jason, "better than nothing. Are you ready?"

"Yeah, I guess so."

"Then let's hope that fucking asshole is still bleeding."

Will gave his brother one last look as they left the office. The expression on his face stayed with him as they left the relative comfort of the gas station and returned to the storm. Isaac looked as though he were having a lovely dream.

* * *

The savagery of the weather was on them before they were even out of the gas station and grew worse the farther they drew away from it. Jason ran, and Will kept up as best he was able, the blood trail coming and going in the same spurts in which it had left its injured former owner. Will found himself following Jason and ignoring the rapidly disappearing trail, stealing glances to the side of the road to see if perhaps whoever had left it had ventured from the streets to find refuge, whether at their intended destination or just one of convenience.

Some of the buildings, Will was able to see from their position in the road, had been shattered by the storm and others left alone. Giant warehouses were torn asunder, while nearby farm-houses remained undisturbed. This was an angry storm, a wind that was attacking at random, and it showed no signs of letting up.

The clothing Will wore was both soaked and frozen, he was cold to the bone, but the only thoughts in his head were of his dead son, the trail of blood, and one foot passing before the other, over and over again. The gloves Jason had handed him just a few impossible hours before were the only thing allowing him to hold onto the carbine, which, for all he knew, wouldn't function in this sort of weather at all.

Will thought of mountain climbers desperate to reach the summit. When asked why, they'd simply say, "Because it's there." He'd always thought that answer was a cheat. Sure the mountain was there, but so was the way around it. Now it occurred to him that walking in the storm to find the man who had killed his son—and maybe also the reason for the death in the first place—was the same as saying, "Because it's there." If asked, Will would have said that he was walking on because he loved Alex, had even loved the stupid things that he had always found himself doing. He loved his son for giving him a reason to live, even as an angry and resentful teen convinced that he was scraping the shit from another man's child.

Alex had become so much more than that, though, just as Will's mother had said that the boy would. The family celebrated Alex's triumphs, and his miscues, as unfortunate as they were, had mostly come after Will's parents had passed. Alex had been a gift given by a woman who had no idea of the wonder of the life she was giving away, a life no less a wonder because its owner had proven, over and over, unable to escape the curse of his blood-line, no matter which tainted father might have been his.

Jason spoke, and the words shook Will from his fugue.

"We need to move more slowly, stay off the road," Jason said, pointing down a path that could have been a six-lane freeway for all Will knew. But still the blood trail was visible in the glow of the few surviving streetlights and occasional bursts of lightning. "They went this way. Let's go see where." Jason launched himself into the snow beside the road, and Will followed him, images of Alex smiling and a smug Chris spitting at Jason alternately rotating in his head.

* * *

They were walking along a driveway now, keeping to the tall pines littering both sides of it. The pines provided dual protection: from prying eyes and from some of the wind and snow. Even in his Thinsulate-lined boots, Will's feet had gone from cold to fire to now just two wooden blocks that were attached somewhere below his knees.

Even Jason was slowing. Will hoped it was the weather wearing him down, and not some additional injury that had been hidden in his clothing. If it was an injury, he knew Jason was a lot more likely to just keel over dead than complain about it. He also knew that he was in no shape to do what remained on his own.

Every few hundred feet of walking in the pines, Jason would loop out so that he could see the road, making sure that they hadn't passed the owner of the blood trail and that they hadn't been doubled back on. After doing this for the fourth time, Jason returned, walking toward Will instead of just continuing forward.

"Looks like they went into a building," he said. "And unless I'm going blind, there's nobody posted by the door." Jason managed a grin, his mouth ringed in ice-crusted facial hair, the cut over his eye caked with snow and fused shut. "The place has taken a beating, but not like some of the shit we've seen. The blood trail ends before it gets to it, or at least it looks that way. We'll see when we get closer."

"Are you ready to do this?" Will asked, not sure if he was ready himself. The snow and the storm had saved them, but it could still be the death of them about as easily as a warehouse full of gangbangers with tattooed faces could be.

"I'm ready," said Jason. "It's only a little further, and then it ends either way. I sure would prefer the winning side, though."

"Hey, at least we should be able to make it inside. Do you think they have heat? Maybe we can dry our boots off before we try and kill each other."

"I think we're lucky just to still be kicking. They got sloppy, should have killed us off at the house, and me being able to take a gun off one of those scary-ass motherfuckers just goes to show that a little more time spent shooting rather than getting their faces all done up might not have been a bad plan."

"Hey, just in case we don't make it out, thanks for your help."

Jason shrugged. "Shit, this is the first worthwhile thing I've done in a long time, even if we have had to torture and kill some people. I feel alive, and my head is clear for once. I'm not going to waste your time with some dumb speech, but this almost makes up for everything else."

"Did you do it?" Once he'd said it, Will wondered where the fuck it had come from. *Now* he was bringing up the girl in the B and E twenty years ago?

But Jason just nodded thoughtfully at him, and when he answered, it was like they were just finishing an interrupted conversation. Like it'd never left his mind. Which it probably hadn't, Will thought.

"I don't know," Jason said. "Isn't that just the most fucked-up thing? If you would have asked me the day after the break-in, I'd have said no. But then, when I got to prison, everybody thought I'd pulled a fast one. My reputation was in place, waiting on me to get there. I never denied it, but it didn't happen the way everybody thinks it did. That's why I was never charged with it, I guess. Bottom line, I didn't put a gun to her head, but I probably had scared the shit out of her, and she felt like she had to do it. Not like it matters, though. No one would ever believe me, and it's fucked up my life enough that, even if they did, there's no fixing what's already happened."

Will wasn't sure what to say to Jason about any of that, and Jason grunted and began moving again before he could come up with anything. Will kept his pace, following his mysterious and damaged friend farther into the trees.

They walked next to each other through the pines, the wind whistling and whipping the branches, distorting sounds so that every cracking branch sounded like a gunshot and everything else eerie and unnatural. The two men were moving at a faster pace than they'd managed since they had left Isaac at the gas station, even through deeper, crusted snow. When they made the edge of the driveway, the warehouse visible to both of them, a few scattered cars in its lot, Will felt almost elated.

They left the tree line, Jason running low and Will mimicking him. The snow before them was speckled with blood again, and Will could see a mess on the door where a great deal of blood had been spilled. He ignored the sickening feeling in his stomach and kept running just behind Jason.

They made the door without seeing any of the MS-13 members, but the storm's racket would have smothered the approach of an armored division on their heels. Hail the size of golf balls had swept after them from the trees, pummeling their backs and the building before them. The metal near the door was warped in spots, as though the building itself had been bent.

Jason turned the knob, and it shocked them both when it turned over. Jason held his finger over his lips. "Shhh."

Will rolled his eyes—like any amount of noise they might make could possibly be heard over the Armageddon coming down on the world—and followed Jason inside, the AR-15 stuck to his shoulder, his right eye looking through the sight and past the reticule, toward possible targets that could appear from nowhere.

The door from outside led into what was basically a kill room. A buffer space meant to stop an attack or raid before it even got started. Bars on the doors, slick walls, a perfect spot to slow an attack, like the spot in a castle before the portcullis but after the moat. Will figured there might be cameras trained on it, but also figured it didn't matter.

Jason moved to the second door. This was the building Chris said he'd been brought to with the hood over his face. It was just as he'd described it: the two doors divided by a short, defensible position so that two doormen could operate separately and help render the normal techniques of a SWAT team useless. Will couldn't see from where he was—the room they were in was lit by just a single lightbulb—but he had a good feeling that there were holes cut high above them to shoot guns and drop grenades into the fishbowl.

Jason turned the second knob, and it was unlocked, just like the first. First Will and then Jason slid into the room, as quietly as they were able.

This room was just as Chris had said as well, though much messier. Blood was all over the room. Across the floor there was a great smear of it, as well as several crimson handprints on the floor, ahead of the smear. Looking at the mess, Will felt a little sick, as though following and chasing death just led to more of the same.

Jason knelt next to the smear, pulled off one glove, and swirled a finger in the mess. "Still warm," he murmured to Will.

"And do you smell the gas? That's why they still have lights, must be running a genny the size of my fucking house to keep a god-damn warehouse lit up."

Jason walked to the next door, looking like he was getting some of his swagger back. Will felt better too. There was pain in his fingers and feet that was almost comforting—pain meant they couldn't have been too damaged, or at least that's what he was hoping. Jason opened the door, even more slowly than he had the last two, and Will followed him through it.

They were in the real warehouse now, though there wasn't much being stored in it. There were a few pallets of boxed high-end electronics—computers, mainly, but also stereo equipment and televisions. Stolen merchandise, Will imagined. He and Jason hugged close to the stacks and peeked around the last one.

There were at least four men inside the warehouse with them.

Three of them looked to be MS-13 members. Two of those were wearing suits, and Will assumed that one of them was the number one man Chris had spoken to earlier. There was a fourth banger lying on his side on the cement floor by the others, and there was blood pooled around him. Will imagined he was prob-ably the one whose draining life had inadvertently led them there. The last man was Chris. He was sitting on a folding chair, and even though Will couldn't see the cocky expression on his face, he felt quite sure that it was there.

Chris was facing away from Will and Jason; the three bangers were facing their way, but cocked away. The man Will assumed was dead was staring at the floor.

Jason slid back and began to move around the row of pallets, farther out of the bangers' line of sight and closer to Chris's. Will followed, listening to the men talking—the bangers in dense Latin accents, Chris repeating something that sounded like, "How long?"

They'd reached the end of the row of pallets and, unless one of the bangers turned, out of the bangers' periphery.

The noise of the hail let up for a moment, and though the wind was still shrieking and making the walls shudder, Will distinctly heard Chris say, "Yeah, but how much longer? No one else can see this shit. I have to give it to him." The hail started again, drowning out whatever response Chris might have gotten.

Will had heard enough, though. The guy who had hired Chris in the first place—the dude who'd ordered the very specific robbery and who may as well have pulled the trigger on Alex himself—wasn't there yet.

Will tapped Wixom's shoulder, and he jumped, whipping around to glare at Will. "Did you hear that?" Will whispered.

"Yeah, big shot ain't here. Storm probably either held him up or killed him."

"So what should we do?"

"Kill them all, then figure out what the fuck is going on. And figure it out somewhere else. This building sounds like it's going to come down around our goddamn ears."

"OK, so let's do it. Try not to hit Chris, the backpack is by his feet, and I still want to see to him myself. Plus, I highly doubt that he's armed."

"All right, I'm in. You take the guy on the left; I'll get the right and then the middle. Before you start moving, lean your rifle against these boxes. They're pretty solid. Shoot through the torso; don't try for the head." Jason took a last look, then turned back to him. "One more thing, there's only the one door, so don't let anyone get to it. Ready?"

* * *

Will placed the dot at the center of the circle over the center of the back of the banger on the left. It would be an easy shot, less than a hundred feet and indoors, so there would be no need to compensate for wind or distance. He just had to leave the dot where it was, let out the air from his lungs, and slowly squeeze the trigger.

It wasn't like aiming at paper, and it wasn't even like shooting Rob had been earlier, when he'd made his dive for his pants. That had been a direct threat; this was quite literally shooting a man in the back.

Will was easing his finger back on the trigger, letting pressure build, on a gun he had never fired before, when, at the exact second that the hammer on his rifle punched the primer on the cartridge, the door they'd entered through opened.

The two men coming in through the door hit the floor and were out of Will's view almost instantly. Jason had dropped his man, and Chris lay on the floor with the backpack next to him. The third banger, the one who Jason had planned to attack second, was firing back at them with a pistol. Will was able to fire at him, but not accurately—it turns out that aiming a gun is quite a bit harder when your target is firing back.

One of the men near the door tried to open it to leave, and Jason volleyed a pair of shots his way, dropping him to the floor, though not from injury. Will tried to get the other banger back in his sights, but the man was running toward the door, making Chris the only living thing still in the middle of the warehouse.

"Chris! Come here!" Will screamed as Jason kept the men by the door honest about keeping their heads and guns down. Chris stood, hesitating for just a moment, and then began to sprint across the warehouse. Neither side was likely much good for him at this point, but there must have been something he saw in Will and Jason that wasn't there in the other three.

Pistol fire bucked from the door, and Jason fired toward the position again, two more quick shots. More pistol fire. Chris was almost to them when blood blossomed on his shirt. He was still moving when he was hit again and slid in a pile next to Will, backpack still in hand.

The blood drained from Chris, his heart pumping away in his chest waiting for the memo that it could take the rest of the day off. He was trying to say something, but the gunfire was too loud and the blood on his lips too thick for Will to make any of it out. A crash of lightning met the occasion of his death, thunder rumbling like cannon fire, and then came a noise unlike anything Will had ever heard before.

The explosion began behind them, Will only realizing that he should move as the lights went out and Jason was grabbing him. They were moving across the building, buffeted by wind and noise as the top of the warehouse was torn off from the ground up and a burst of flame roared across the floor, shooting up in great blasts of blue fire from cracks and holes in the cement floor.

What was left of the door was covered in flames, the door frame itself collapsing. Jason kept driving toward the door, ignoring the flames and dragging Will with him. *He's going to kill us*, Will thought in a flash of hallucinatory clarity as the flames engulfed the world around them, and then it was Will who was pulling Jason, away from the door and the fire, to the wall opposite of their shooting position.

"Wrong way, Will!" Jason screamed, but the voice was small in Will's head, and he ignored the words, continuing to haul Jason like an ornery calf toward a wall while the fire built around them, burning hotter by the second and stealing the oxygen from his lungs.

There was a smell within the flames—an odor of burning chemicals and something almost euphoric Will had a hard time figuring out—but he didn't hate the smell, it was just overpowering. Jason shoved him around a blast of purple flame that appeared from the concrete to Will's left, and then there was nothing in front of them but a wall. Will put his left hand on Jason's shoulder, the AR still clutched in his right, and shoved him into the wall, directly into a square of aluminum divided by two steel beams. Jason flew into it without resistance, Will jumping behind him into it.

\* \* \*

Jason landed in the snow, and Will fell next to him. An aluminum panel from the warehouse wall was smoldering underneath them, and Will rolled away from the heat to the surprising comfort of the wet snow.

The flames had scorched his coat, taken the hair from his head. His eyebrows and scalp felt raw and sticky and chafed in the wind.

As noise from the collapsing building continued, Jason stood, looking to Will like some Viking warrior. Smoke poured off his smoldering friend, the wind and ruins of the building adding to the picture, as Jason shouldered the AK-47 and fired four shots into the retreating black Cadillac SUV. Then the magazine was empty, the last round left the barrel, and the bolt locked back, ready for a new magazine. Jason dropped the gun and grabbed Will by what remained of the back of his coat, forcing him to stand.

"OK, OK," Jason said, grabbing his knees. "Time to get our shit togeth—"

An explosion from behind them sent both men staggering forward. Chunks of the building were going everywhere, and the storm was still exploding around them.

When things had settled down, at least as far as the disintegrating building was concerned, Jason turned to him. "Will, this is going to suck, but we need to get back to your brother and that gas station. Can you help me?"

"Sure. What's wrong?"

Jason collapsed in his arms then, blood gurgling from his mouth, more body heat rolling off his torso than Will could believe. He set his friend down onto the ground and saw for the first time that somehow Jason had taken Chris's backpack from the burning building. Will took and shouldered the backpack, then ran back toward the building, back to where they'd left the chunk of aluminum from the wall that he'd shoved Jason through. He dragged it back to Jason, rolled his friend onto the metal, and slapped him, the man's eyes coming alive with rage. Will lay his stolen AR-15 on Jason's chest.

"You've got to stay awake," said Will. "You hold this while I pull you out of here, you got that?"

Jason grunted something indistinguishable, and Will slapped him again. Jason's eyes came back iron, flecked with green and gold. "You hit me again," he said, "and I'll kill you."

"You fall asleep again, I'll leave you for dead."

"Fuck you."

"Fuck you right back," said Will, pulling the makeshift sled through the snow. "Fuck you very much. Keep that gun ready, you fucker."

"Fuck you," said Jason as Will moved them up the driveway. "This is all your fault."

"You're the one that knocked her up," said Will, "I guarantee it. Now stop telling me to fuck off, and make sure that Caddy doesn't come back. Bitch."

"Fuck you," said Jason, lucid now, or at least somewhat. "Damn my head hurts, Will."

"I know, mine too. What the fuck was in that place?" He shook his head, loosing a fresh wave of pain. "Doesn't matter. I'm getting us back to Isaac."

"I've got your back."

**W**ill's arms were freezing. Everything else was too, but the cold was the worst in his arms. Jason was having an on-again, off-again battle with lucidity, and Will was no longer just scared that the tattooed ex-con might shoot him in the back, he was expecting it. If anything, he was shocked it had taken so long to happen.

Every slogging step through the slush and snow was hell, every gust of wind a knee-buckling hurricane, every noise terrifying. Will had no idea what time it was, no idea how much farther the gas station was, or if there was even any point to dragging Jason there. If his wounds were too bad, there was nothing he was going to be able to do about them, not on his own and certainly not with the supplies he'd be limited to in the battered Sunoco. Still, Will continued dragging the alternately babbling and snoring Jason behind him and just tried to worry about the step he was taking, not the one after it.

When the gas station finally came into sight, Will was sure he was just imagining things, but he pushed on.

It was the real deal. And Will smelled smoke. Christ, had he made it all the way there only to watch the fucker burn?

As he dragged Jason into the gas station's fueling area, he saw that his nose hadn't betrayed him: smoke was billowing from the gas station. Forgetting Jason, Will ran to the building and to his brother.

"Isaac!" Will screamed as he crunched over the broken glass, then slowed, then stopped. The smoke was coming from a fire set in the middle of the service area's floor. The office door opened, and Isaac was walking toward him.

"Will, holy shit. Thank God. Where's Jason? And what the fuck happened to you?"

"He's outside. Can you help me get him?"

"I can use my left arm," said Isaac, pointing with his left arm to his right, which was tied up in a homemade sling, "but I'm pretty sure this one's broken."

"That's fine. Just help me bring him in."

Will left the gas station with his brother in tow and found Jason lying flat on his back in the snow atop the makeshift sled. Ignoring his brother's questioning look, Will grabbed a piece of the sled and began pulling, while Isaac attempted to do the same on his side. After just a few moments, Jason had been moved to the doorway, and Will slipped the gun from his fingers, then slung it over his shoulders.

"Let's pick him up," Will said. "You get on his right side; I'll be on the left." Will moved into position, his right arm under Jason's left, and wrapped around his upper back. Will felt Isaac doing similar maneuvering, and then his brother grabbed his forearm. "You ready?"

"Yeah, I think so."

"All right, three, two, one."

The brothers stood with Jason between them and slowly entered the gas station, trying to keep Jason's face away from the smoke, as well as their own. They knelt with him a few feet from the fire, and Will took off what was left of his coat to give Jason a place to lay his head.

"Goddamn, that fire feels nice," Will said. "Where'd you get all the wood?"

"There was a bunch out back," said Isaac, grinning. "All split, packaged, and ready for sale. I figured that stealing it was a minor party foul, considering all of the other insurance work these poor bastards are going to see."

Will walked to the back of the store and helped himself to a bottle of water from one of the broken coolers. He unscrewed the lid and took a drink, then spit onto the floor. The fluid that came from his mouth was black, with chunks in it. He repeated the act three more times, then blew his nose, farmer style, onto the floor, pinching off one nostril and blowing, then doing the other side.

"Make yourself at home," said Isaac, "but if you could avoid shitting on the floor, that would be great."

Perusing an aisle of snacks that had been blown on the floor, Will said, "No promises." He left the snacks, figuring the water was good enough for a start, and walked back to Jason. He was in rough shape, Will could tell that by just looking at him. He knelt next to the prone body, unslinging his AR-15 and laying it on the floor. He slid Jason's left arm from his jacket, and then the right. Will rolled his friend's shirt up, cringing at what he saw.

Jason's left side was black with bruising, and his ribs rose and fell in weirdly disordered hills and valleys that brought the words *multiple fracture* to Will's mind. His breathing was hitched, normal enough on the right side, but labored on his savaged left side.

"Christ," Isaac said. "Looks like your buddy punctured his lung. That's not good."

"No, it isn't. When was the last time you checked the land line in the office?"

"Only about every ten minutes since I woke up. Fill me in. The last thing I remember, we got tricked somehow and were getting into a van with a bunch of bastards. Did they have tattooed faces, or was that just a bad dream?"

"No," said Will, taking a drink of water and keeping it down this time, "not a dream. Bunch of gangbangers from something called MS-Thirteen kidnapped us and were bringing us out here to die. The storm got to be too much for the driver, and Jason got to be too much for just about everybody. When I woke up, he was killing people left and right, and I dragged you out of the wreck."

"Nice of you."

"No problem. Hell, Jason did most of the work. He got rid of the rest of the bastards, got us both guns, and then carried you here. The note was my idea."

"Nice touch."

"Thanks. Anyways, after that, we went to go see where that bastard Chris had gone off to—he wasn't in the van when I woke up. We followed his blood trail—really, Jason followed it, and I followed him—and then we got the drop on them. We were just about to finish it, kill the bad guys, get the gold, and get out of there, when two more of them came in the room, the leader of the tattoo faces and some suit—I didn't get a good look at him. Everybody started shooting everybody else, and then the whole place just blew apart."

"Meth lab," said Jason from the floor, making both brothers jump. His voice was raspy, like his throat was full of glass, but he seemed much more lucid than he had while Will was dragging him to the Sunoco.

"What do you mean, meth lab?" Will asked.

Jason said, "Water."

Will knelt, unscrewed the lid from the bottle, and poured some water into Jason's mouth. Jason promptly turned his head and spit on the floor—black chunks, just like when Will had done the same thing. Jason nodded, and Will repeated the act, four more times in total.

Jason took the bottle from Will then and splashed some water in his face, then eyed Will. "Christ, you look about like I feel. Might be best to avoid mirrors and the public for a few months."

"What were you saying about a meth lab?" Isaac asked, and Jason nodded.

"The place we got in the gunfight in was set on top of a meth lab. My guess would be that lightning hit the generator, and they were cooking down there. Place went up like a fucking fireball.

I bet it's still burning. Probably the craziest thing I've ever seen. How'd we get back here?"

"I dragged you on a piece of the building."

"Bullshit. You?"

"It's true," said Isaac. "I saw him do it."

"I'd say thanks, but I imagine you still owe me for a couple, minimum."

"I'm not going to dispute that."

"So what's the plan now?" Jason asked. "We gonna call somebody for help? I imagine our bad-guy-wrangling days are over."

"No phones," said Will. "They took ours, remember? Plus the land line here is still dead, might be that way for days."

"How about one of them?"

"What?"

"One of those ones," said Jason, struggling to point to a display behind the register. "Get one a them burners, turn one on, register it, and call home. You can call my girl at the tattoo shop if you want; she'll haul us home on her back if I tell her there's some blow in it for her."

"Nice girl," Will agreed, "but I think I'll try my wife first, assuming that's OK with you."

\* \* \*

It took Will more than a few minutes of fumbling to get the phone out of the package, registered, and dialing home, but when Alison answered, it was all worth it.

"Hello?" she answered, her voice drawn tight as wire. Even though it was not quite morning yet, Will could tell she hadn't been sleeping.

"It's Will, hon. Are you doing OK? I'm sorry it took so long for me to call."

"Goddamn you, Will Daniels! Goddamn you. I'm so glad you're OK, but last night was the worst, the absolute worst. Is everything OK?"

Will caught himself appraising Jason and then Isaac before answering. "Things have been better, how's that for a start?"

"It'll do, I guess. Did you…do what you set out to do?"

"Yes and no. It's a long story. It's been pretty terrible out, and I hate to ask, but if you could try to come get us, we'd love to tell it to you."

"Of course I'll come get you. Wait, where are you?"

"Right now, we're hiding out in a gas station off of the Fruitridge exit on the—"

"Jesus Christ! Are you serious? Do you have any idea how bad the storm was out there last night? Whole buildings were ruined. The pictures make it look like spring in tornado alley."

"Were there tornados?"

"No, the weather has been calling it 'straight-line winds,' whatever that means. I'm going to fetch my keys and get out there. I'll call if I get lost."

"Don't you have to get dressed?"

"I've been waiting for the call that you'd been arrested or killed. I still have my shoes on. I love you. I'll be there soon."

The receiver went dead, and out of habit, Will stuck the phone in his pocket. "She's coming to get us, leaving right now."

"Great," said Jason. "I can't wait to not explain what happened to me tonight in the prison wing of the hospital." He stopped then and gave them a confused look. "Hey, what was in that goddamn bag, after all?"

Will looked at the forgotten pack on the floor near the counter, then walked over and grabbed it and brought it back to Jason. Isaac chose to sit next to them as well, as Will unzipped the bag, feeling like a poisonous snake or some other awful demon was going to leap out of it.

When he finally stuck his hand inside, all there was to pull out was a thin manila envelope with a sealed top.

"Open the fucker," said Jason, and that's what Will did.

\* \* \*

Will emptied the contents of the envelope onto his lap.

The manila envelope held three glossy eight-by-ten prints. Will turned the first one over. It was a color picture taken from inside of a hotel room, and in the picture, a young girl, not much older than ten, was crying while she performed oral sex on a man in his early fifties or late sixties. Will thought he might recognize the man, but couldn't place him. His already upset stomach now roiling, Will passed the picture to Jason, who let Isaac lean in to see.

"Shit," said Jason. "That is seriously fucked up."

Will turned over the next picture. In this one, the man was penetrating the girl from behind, and at some point between the taking of the first and second picture, a ball gag had been placed in her mouth, and her right eye had been blackened. Makeup was running down her face and so was a trail of blood, leaking from her right nostril. Will passed the picture on and flipped over the next one.

In the last shot, the man's smiling, glistening face was clear as day, though Will could hardly believe it was really him. The rest of the picture was too much for Will to look at. He set it on his lap, facedown, and then passed it to Jason.

After just a moment, Jason confirmed what Will had been thinking when he said, "Holy fuck. That's the goddamn mayor, and he killed that kid."

"Are you serious?" Isaac asked. "Is that really the fucking mayor?"

That any of them could recognize Mayor Robert Huntington at all would normally have been pretty unlikely—none of them were exactly civic-minded—but the last mayoral election had been brutal, fought over the airwaves for months by two parties all too happy to leverage the country's toxic national-level partisanship at the local level. Mayor Huntington had been the incumbent and was running for his fourth term, but the once esteemed man had had his name absolutely dragged through the mud. The tales of corruption went so deep that it seemed no one on the Kent County political scene could be clean. A new mayor seemed the obvious solution—until, that is, the man running against Huntington, one Judd Foster, was arrested for DUI just a week before the election, with a passenger that was not his wife.

That had scotched his election chances, of course. Huntington won in a landslide, even with his reputation destroyed in the doing. Since then, he had been aggressively quashing any lingering or new allegations of corruption and using the police force as a club to do it with, at least according to his opposition. There had been no outcry among the honest citizenry, at least not yet, largely because of Huntington's unexpected success in bringing the local drug trade to heel. Meth and cocaine had all but disappeared from the streets, and it was presumed that there wasn't a gang in the city not hobbled by an informant at some level.

That was about to change, Will figured, and these photos were the reason. It surprised him, especially given how exhausted and beaten up he was, how quickly it snapped into focus for him. He could, of course, be all wrong, but he didn't think so, at least not in the big picture. The photos had been taken, God only knew why (trophies for their psychopath of a mayor to gaze upon and whack off to?), and then they'd fallen into the hands of some unknown entrepreneur and shopped around. MS-13 had put in their bid—and then decided to cut to the front of the line and snatch them, once they figured out (or were told) where they were hidden away. Whoever had the pics would have an ax over Huntington's neck plenty sharp enough to step in and fill the city's drug vacuum without fear of police interference—or thanks to the success of the recent crackdown, even an ounce of competition.

Jason was running some at least similar calculus in his head, it turned out. "I say we burn them," he said. "Just pitch them right into the fire. They won't do nothing but get us killed, and I've been almost killed enough for a good little while."

Will shook his head. "The little girl in these pictures is dead, and we're the only people who can do anything about it."

"Only if you can figure out how to breathe life back into her. This song and dance has worn me pretty thin. We've done just about everything we could to get that goddamn package, and now that we've got it, I'll be damned if it still kills me. No one knows we have it. I guarantee those guys think we died in the fire at the warehouse, and they sure as hell think these pictures are long gone."

"But we know that they're not," reasoned Will. "We have a chance to make this as close to right as possible."

"Will, be reasonable," said Isaac. "We've already gone to hell and back over Alex and that backpack. I think Jason's right; it's over. Jason needs to get to the hospital, and so do I. Just put them in the fire, and live the rest of your life forgetting that you ever saw them. I know I will. It's for the best."

A horn honking in front of the gas station interrupted them, and Will took the distraction to stuff the pictures into the backpack and then dropped the AR-15 on top of them. Isaac was helping Jason stand, and Will slung the pack over his shoulder, then made a show of dropping the empty file into the fire.

"Happy?"

"Yes," said Jason and Isaac at the same time.

Will followed them outside, where Alison was waiting for them in her car. Morning was finally coming.

* * *

Alison looked shocked as Will and Isaac helped Jason into the car, and remained that way as Isaac sat in the back and Will took a seat next to her in the front. The clock in the center of the dash had the time, 7:15 a.m. Just looking at the clock made Will dizzy, but his eyes were drawn to it, as if to remind him that everything really had happened, and there was going to be no reprieve in realizing that any of it had been a dream or that perhaps his mind had exaggerated what had happened to them. Some part of him even wished that he had put the pictures to the flame and that this really was the end.

"I said, what happened, Will?" Alison said, nearly shouting. "What in the hell happened last night? You smell like a campfire gone wrong, and you look terrible."

"We can explain as we go," Will said. "Just drive."

She scowled, the car still sitting in park.

"Please. Drive."

Alison put the car in drive, then pulled out of the gas station. Will thought he could still see some blood on the road but didn't say anything. It wasn't important anymore.

"I'm not really mad," said Alison. "At least, I don't think I am. But I was really worried. Why didn't you call?"

"Well, I should have, around ten thirty, before the shit really hit the fan, but—"

"They took our phones," offered Jason, "right about at ten thirty, if memory serves."

"Who took your phones?"

"MS-Thirteen is what I figured," said Jason, and Isaac agreed with a nod of his head. "They certainly had the war paint to at least run a good impression of MS-Thirteen."

"Who or what is MS-Thirteen?"

"A gang that started in El Salvador," Will explained. "They hired Alex and his friends—Chris, Mumbo, and Rob—to rob a bank for them."

"Only, they weren't really just robbing a bank," offered Isaac. "They were trying to steal some pictures to use as blackmail. There's a lot we still don't get just yet."

"I believe you," said Alison. "I can see how some of the intimate details of the situation may have escaped you guys. Are they dead?"

"Most of them," Will said. "The kids who were with Alex when he died all are, most of the MS-Thirteen guys we ran into are as well, and we destroyed the pictures they wanted, to boot."

"Are they going to be able to find you?"

"No," said Jason from the back. They hit a bump in the road then, and he said, "Oof. Christ, that stings." He took a breath, then went on. "The only ones that seen us are dead, and the ones that didn't I think are happy just to get gone. We blew up their meth lab."

"You blew up the Salvadoran gang's meth lab." Alison said this like she was just checking.

"The weather did that," said Will. "We just happened to be there."

"I changed my mind," she said. "I can hear the rest whenever Will feels like telling me about it, but I'm in no rush. Why don't you guys take a look out the windows, get a gander at how jacked up everything was? You guys might have busted up a few parties, but that storm took out half of the north end."

It was true. Looking out of the car window and actually trying to see what was going on was incredibly unnerving, as the realization that a gang of bloodthirsty killers had been maybe the least of their worries began to hit home.

The storm had not just forced two vans to crash, destroyed a gas station, and blown up a warehouse-turned-gang-hideout/ meth lab. It had also ravaged a number of houses visible from the highway, destroyed several warehouses (Will was sure that one they saw was the warehouse he'd seen being shredded just before the van crashed), among many other ruined buildings. The storm had laid waste to a barn's worth of cattle; a hundred or more head of dead cows lay strewn about a field, and a long-horned bull was atop a farmhouse, upside down and quite dead. The *Grand Rapids Press* printing facility was the only thing that Will saw that seemed completely untouched, and as they drove past it, he saw that even the *Press* had been hit: the cars in its parking lot had all been smashed into each other, the pavement, and the building.

Will closed his eyes as Alison drove and fell asleep before they crossed under Alpine Avenue.

* * *

Will started as Alison shook him, then sat up straight in the seat. She'd pulled over along the road just outside the city, maybe half a mile from the hospital. The neighborhood visible to him looked absolutely untouched by the storm. It looked as phony as a movie set.

Alison was smiling at him, a thing Will had been quite positive was never going to happen again, and he smiled back. She squeezed his knee, and he felt like everything might be OK. When the look broke, he turned to see into the backseat; Isaac and Jason were as asleep as he had been.

"I wanted to check," Alison said, "before we get to the hospital. What do you want to happen?"

Will thought about her, his friends, and the contents of the backpack. "Drive to the hospital. I'll leave you there with the guys. I need to go talk to Lou. I need to run some of this by him."

"What do you think he'll say?"

"To be perfectly honest, I have no idea. But we need to have our ducks in a row. The police are going to release Alex to us soon, and we need to be ready to take care of that and act like everything is perfectly normal."

"What should I tell the hospital about these two idiots?"

"Say Isaac's your brother-in-law, and he got hurt in the storm. On the way to the hospital, you found Jason hitchhiking, and he was all beat up too. Or anything else that makes better sense to you. Anything but the truth, really. I'd stay as far away from that as possible."

"That is not going to be a problem."

"I had a feeling. No matter what, don't answer any questions from the police that you aren't one hundred percent on. There are going to be a lot of people fucked up from the storm in there with them, so let that be the cause of it. No reason to get fancy or hung up on details. These two have enough sense to lie their asses off. When you get inside, just make sure that the only story they have is that they were hurt in the storm and don't know how."

"You really think that will be good enough?"

"Normally, no," said Will, grinning. "But that storm wasn't normal. It could give even the most normal person a horrible night."

"All right," she said, sighing. "One more thing, though, don't grin like that anymore, not until your hair grows back. It makes you look really creepy."

"I've been lucky enough to avoid mirrors thus far."

"I would keep that up for as long as you're able."

"Done."

"Will, I know what you did was stupid, and dangerous, and that you probably ought to be dead, but I'm still glad you did it."

"Me too," he said, trying not to think about the carbine in the backpack or the pictures hidden with it. "Me too."

The rest of the drive went smoothly, ending as Alison parked the car in front of the hospital, then running inside to see about some wheelchairs for Isaac and Jason. Will turned in his seat and smacked their legs until they were awake. Isaac looked like he wanted to kill him; Jason looked like he wanted to kill him, resurrect him, and then kill him again. Will gave them the grin he'd been counseled to avoid and said, "Rise and shine. We're at the hospital."

"Fuck you," said Jason in a contented voice before closing his eyes and leaning against the window.

"I'm serious," said Will. "Get up."

Jason shook himself awake and gave Will a fresh dirty look.

"Alison will be back any second. If you guys have to talk to the cops, just say you got hurt in the storm. Listen to what Alison says and stick to that story. Deny knowing one another, just take as many easy questions as possible, don't get frustrated, and act as medicated as possible. Got it?"

They both bobbled their heads at him, and then Alison and four orderlies were there to unload his brother and friend. Before Will knew it, they were out of the car, and Alison was waving to him in the rearview mirror.

---
　　　　　　　　　　　🚹🚹🚹
---

**W**ill drove himself toward Lou's office and, as an afterthought, took the cell phone from his pocket. Momentarily confused when he flipped it open and stared at the unfamiliar controls, he couldn't help but laugh when he realized his problem. As helpful as it would have been for the person most likely to carry a burner to have a lawyer like Lou's on their contact list, this particular phone was not so equipped. *This is the stupidest thing in the world*, Will thought. *I don't know any phone numbers off of the top of my head.* Making a mental note to go to his cell phone provider to see about a replacement phone at some point in the near future, he drove the rest of the way to Lou's office in silence. It was wonderful.

Will pulled in next to Lou's black Cadillac Escalade, parked in its usual spot in the lot. He got out, closing Alison's car door, and then walked around the rear of the car to open the front passenger door and retrieve his backpack, still full with three horrible pictures and the loaded rifle. Will hefted the bag, briefly considering offloading the rifle and then reconsidering the idea. Lou would be as good a person as any to ask what he should do with the stolen and likely illegal weapon. Crossing the parking lot, Will caught himself smiling. This was almost over.

The door to the office was open, even though the sign said they wouldn't be open until 9:00 a.m., and it was barely 8:00. Will walked past the always-empty secretary's desk and knocked on Lou's office door.

"Hello?" Will called. "Lou, this is Will Daniels. I have some stuff I need to run by you, if you're not too busy."

"C'mon in, Will," called Lou from behind the door.

Will opened the door. The office was immaculate, but Lou looked awful behind his desk. The lawyer was disheveled, suit in disarray, hair every which way—not at all like Lou, or at least the Lou that Will knew. What the hell, he figured, last night had been a rough night all around the city. He walked and slid into one of Lou's comfortable chairs.

"Everything OK, Lou? You're here awful early."

"I could ask you the same thing," Lou said. "You look like you got run over by a truck, and half of your hair's been burnt off. I've been here all night, as it happens. Tell the truth, I hardly ever leave these days." Lou pinched his nose shut and chuckled. "And I didn't mention the smell yet. Shit, Will, what the hell happened?"

"Long story," said Will, sighing. "A very long story. But here's the short of it: I've got some pictures I need you to look at. I think it's in your best interests that you not know how I got them or who I took them from."

Lou gave him a long look. "These don't sound like they're going to be pictures of a trip to Disney World, Will. Hell, they don't sound like pictures from a trip to anywhere somebody might like to go at all. What are they of?"

"I'd rather not say," said Will, his stomach rolling at the thought of them. "Honestly, I'm not going to look at them again, either. I imagine that you'll feel the same way when you see them."

Will opened the backpack between his legs, moved the short rifle from atop the pictures, took the photos from the bag, and slid them facedown across the table. Lou picked the first one off of the stack, his eyes bugging out of his head and then relaxing. He set the photo down and picked up the second one.

"Is this who I think it is?" Lou asked, and Will just nodded. Lou set the picture down and picked up the third photo, shaking his head. "It's enough to make you want to puke. What do you expect me to do with these, Will?"

"Honestly, Lou, I have no idea. I suppose what ought to happen is they wind up with the police, but I've been through enough trouble to come by them that I can see how that might not be a safe option. There seem to be a number of people who have invested a great deal of time and energy into getting these, or getting rid of them, and I want my involvement with them to cease. I think it would be best for the community if the mayor saw prison over this, but I have no idea if that's even possible."

"You let me worry about that, Will. I can handle all the details; that's what I'm here for. Let me make some phone calls, fish around a little bit. Could be the police cannot be trusted in this matter, either. I do know a couple of guys on the force. I got a captain that I go way back with. Maybe I'll see what he has to say. I think the play here is to insinuate, not offer. Suggest that I heard something instead of saying, 'Look what I got.' Even with all the corruption I've seen in local government, this one takes the cake. It's a new level, even for our mayor."

"Thanks, Lou. This really helps, man. With everything else going on, all the stuff with Alex, this mess was the last thing I needed to be involved with. I just wanted some answers, but the shit got too deep for me, too deep by a long shot."

"Rest easy, buddy, this is easy from here on out. I make some calls, and this either disappears or a real fucking mess hits this town. I'll keep your name out of it."

Lou stood, extending a hand, and Will stood as well, taking Lou's hand into his own and shaking it. They released the grip, and Will knelt, zipped the bag up, and stood.

"I'll be in touch," said Lou. "Count on it."

"I am, but if you hear from me first, come running. I stirred up some shit last night. I think I'm good on most of it, but if I do call, it's going to be with a real mess stuck to my shoes."

"Don't sweat it. Let it all go. Shit, go write. I'm sure they'll release Alex soon, so you'll be busy enough to avoid worrying too much. Besides, the cops aren't exactly knocking down your door, are they?"

"Not yet."

"So forget about them. Take care of your family. Go live. I'll talk to you soon."

* * *

Will felt good leaving Lou's office. The man might not be the best lawyer, but a guy could sure as hell do worse. Leaving the pictures with him felt good. If Lou trashed them, that just meant that there was no possibility of redemption for that poor little girl, nor was there a possibility of punishment for the man who had killed her. Still, handing it over to Lou gave it a chance that it wouldn't have had relying on Will's abilities alone. All he would have done was fumble things, make it worse for himself and his family, and still done nothing for the girl.

Will took the cell phone from his pocket, slowly dialing Alison's number as he walked past Lou's SUV. Hers was one of the few that he knew by heart. She answered on the third ring, and he stopped walking.

"Hello?"

"Hey, babe, it's me. Weird number, remember?"

"That phone sounds like crap."

"Well, I did steal it from a gas station. If anything, it's amazing that the battery is still kicking. When you really think about it, you're lucky to be talking to me."

"Believe me, I'm counting my blessings about that."

"Good, I'm glad. How are the boys?"

"Isaac is OK. His right arm is broken in at least two spots, and the doctor said that before the X-ray."

"He call Daisy yet?"

"No, and he forbid me from calling her. I'm still obeying the ruling, but my resolve is cracking."

"Do your best. How's Jason?"

Will could hear her take a deep breath, then let it out slowly, trying to make it so he couldn't hear it. "He's not good. From what I could gather as a nonfamily member, he's in really bad shape. His rib cage is basically shattered on one side, and he's got a ton of damage to the lung, multiple perforations. I'm pretty sure he was shot, too, but they don't talk about that."

"He was shot? Do you know where?"

"No, but I assume lower body. I heard a doctor talking about his leg."

"Hell, I guess we're all lucky we got out of there at all." He sighed, finding he'd made a decision to tell her a little more. "Babe, don't tell those guys, but I lied a little bit to them. They thought I got rid of some stuff we found, but I brought it to Lou, to see if he couldn't make heads or tails of it, anyways—"

Will had turned in the parking lot as he'd spoken, but now his words stuck in his throat. His eyes were locked onto Lou's SUV. There was no snow on Lou's Escalade, not a drop of ice, yet he said he'd been there all night. More than that, three bullet holes were visible in the tailgate.

"Oh fuck," said Will, remembering Jason firing after the fleeing black Cadillac SUV the night before, four shots. Jason had missed once, it seemed.

Will looked up. Lou was walking toward him, struggling with a jacket pocket, arguing with the fabric for something that he seemed to need very badly.

"I have to go," said Will, watching a nickel-plated wheel gun pull free from Lou's coat, then turning away from his lawyer, speaking loudly. "We need to go over my new contract."

"What new contract?" Alison said, puzzled, as Lou pushed the revolver against the back of his head.

"My new book and the new contract Jack got for me," said Will, the gun against his skull, the phone feeling like a piece of dust in his fingers, the rifle in the backpack a weight, but a million miles away. "I told you about that."

"Hang up now," said Lou. "Right now."

"All right, Lou's off the horn now. We'll see what Terri had to say."

Will was able to hear one word as the burner came off of his ear, and it was, "Cops?"

"Yes, baby," said Will as Lou pushed the gun into his head. "Love you, too." He closed the phone and tucked it into his pocket, then let Lou push him inside.

* * *

"Goddamn it, Will," said Lou as he walked Will back into the office, "you were never supposed to be involved. This is all just a damn mess now. What in the fuck were you thinking?"

"I just wanted to see some justice for Alex, that was it. But the more I dug, the worse it got."

Lou shoved Will roughly into the chair he'd been in earlier, and then Lou sat in his own chair across from him, keeping his gun on Will as he moved. Will took the backpack off, watching the revolver barrel the whole time and thinking about the gun inside the bag, the AR-15 as far away as a well-meaning buddy stuck in Timbuktu. Lou shook his head as though he'd heard a funny joke, then frowned.

"So what now, Will?" Lou asked. "What in the hell am I supposed to do with you? These pictures were supposed to be sold, and you went and fucked everything up. It's bad enough nothing like this turned up before the election, when my guy, the fucking idiot, could've used the help. Now you fucked up the deal I *was* able to manage. All you had to do was just let it go. This was finished. It was over. And don't think I'm such a bad guy, either."

"Oh, no, Lou. You're a prince."

"Shut the fuck up. All I did was get the word that there were some pictures out there and made some calls. Carlos and his nasty little buddies came through. MS-Thirteen gets a bad rap, the way he tells it. Other gangs will unite just to try and get rid of them, but that's like putting out a fire by filling your dick with gas and commencing to piss on the flames—it doesn't even sound good in theory. These people are not to be fucked with, not with their money and especially not personally. You've done both."

"I know that. How do we make this right?"

"We don't, Will. Or at least, we don't for you. I tend to land on my feet. You look to be on life *numero nueve*, as our friends from El Salvador might say. Come on now, stand up. And leave that fucking backpack where it is. I can tell by the way you're hanging onto it that you've got a piece in there."

Will stood, casting a brief, mournful look at the backpack. It was his last link to survival; he was losing the strings that connected him with life by the second. Lou slid open a pocket door that Will had often noticed but never seen the other side of, and Lou ushered him in with his left arm, the one without the heater. Will walked through the door and stopped, almost falling backward.

The room had no windows, but did have a second door. That one wore a padlock. There was a sink, a toilet, and a man lying on a Murphy bed on the far side of the room. The man had tattoos all over his face, and he wore a very well-tailored suit, the right side of the coat soiled with a round, red spot the size of a small pizza. It was no longer very wet, so maybe he was no longer bleeding. But the man's ochre pallor told the tale—gut shot, and badly.

The wounded man barked something in Spanish, and Lou pulled off his second trick of the day, responding in kind before turning to Will.

"Your friend shot this man," he said. "I'm guessing it happened when we were driving away. I saw you admiring the scars on the Caddy out front, putting the pieces together. One of those bullets drove through my friend, my partner on this deal. He lost a stable manufacturing business, a lot of friends, and he's at least a day away from the sort of doctor he needs."

"That's a tough spot. Can't say I'll lose sleep over it, though. That's the asshole that got my son killed."

"No," said Lou, "your son came in on a job and got nosy, that's why he's got a toe tag. You came looking for what happened, but your ego never let you see that everything around you was bigger than your want to see justice. Your son killed people, he robbed people—he got what he gave to another man just minutes before. He made you into a lunatic."

Will considered that, giving a look to the waiting-to-die MS-13 leader and then back to Lou and his gun.

"How long have you been living here, Lou?"

"A long time, Will. A very long time. That last divorce destroyed me. I tried to hint around about that, but you never seemed too interested. This was a way out of that, a perfect one. Crack the mayor open on the street like a rotten egg and get paid for doing it."

"Lou, you were fucking her best friend. What was she supposed to do?"

"An affair should have nothing to do with alimony. No judge could ever make me believe otherwise, and you won't, either. Not that it matters. I'm broke, and what can you do about that?"

"You heard me talking to Alison, about a new contract?"

"Yes. So what? You were just bullshitting me. You're a two-time lucky hack that managed to get off the sauce long enough to write the denouement of your own life. Nothing more."

"Yeah, OK. Maybe. So you're fucked on money. I guess this is just the end of it."

The man on the foldout bed groaned loudly and began to piss blood onto the floor, the moan turning high-pitched, and as Lou lowered the gun to frown in disgust at the smell of urine and death, Will charged him, all fear gone. The revolver barked once as Will hit him.

\* \* \*

Will landed with Lou under him and began smashing his fists against him as fast as he was able. Lou had fired once, and Will hadn't felt anything, at least not yet. The wounded man on the foldout was screaming in a language that Will wasn't sure he would've understood even with a fluency in Spanish.

Will connected with Lou's nose, hard enough to feel the cartilage shift under his hand and to force a high-pitched squeal from his attorney. Will could feel Lou trying to turn under him, and he brought his elbow down in a point to attack Lou's ribs, eliciting more pained noises.

He rose up to punch Lou again. He was starting to like the way using his hands on the lawyer felt; it was an adrenaline dump strong enough to make him forget that he was exhausted. He cocked his fist, and something smashed into the back of his head, toppling him, and the world faded from gray to black, then drifted back to gray.

Will was on his hands and knees. He could see Lou next to him, slowly attempting to stand, the revolver blindly menacing the room as he wobbled. The MS-13 leader was staggering across the room, hanging onto a piece of the chair he'd used to smash Will with before collapsing next to the Murphy, the wound to his side more than doubled now and leaking blood so congealed that it had the consistency of strawberry jam. Will watched Lou stand, slowly, the pistol rising, and Will drove his body into his legs, the gun going off again.

Will assumed that the second shot from the revolver must have hit the banger, because he still felt no gunshot wound, but the gangster was screaming. Not the whimpering that he was doing when his bladder loosed itself, but really howling now. Will wanted to tell him to stop, to please just shut up, to ask Lou to stop, that they could work something out. He knew that was impossible, though, so instead of holding up a white handkerchief, Will held Lou's right wrist with his left, the revolver moving back and forth, up and down, over his face and then away from it. Will slipped his right fist past Lou's left to try and punch him again, but the lawyer saw it coming, and when Will shifted his weight to add leverage to the shot, Lou bucked his hips. Will fell off of him, and Lou stood. Blood was dripping from his mouth, and he started to raise the revolver. If there was a soul behind Lou's eyes, Will couldn't see it.

"You fuck! You broke my nose!" Lou shouted, barely loud enough to be heard over the screaming from the dying man. Lou walked over to the banger, seeming to consider the screaming man, and shot him in the head. The gunshot was deafening, but then the room was silent. Then he turned back to Will. "I wish I could let you walk away, Will, but you know I can't."

Will watched from ten feet away as the revolver was pointed at his legs, chest, and finally, his face. There was an explosion, and the world went to black and stayed there this time.

**W**ill found himself sitting on a beach. He had no idea where, and then he saw the bridge, the Mac. He stood, feeling sand between the toes of his bare feet, and began scanning his environment.

Save for a man a few hundred feet away down the beach, closer to the bridge, he was alone. Will was drawn to the man like a junkie to a bag of white powder and began walking toward him, and at the exact same time, the man began to walk in his direction. As the man got closer, Will came to the realization that he knew him. As they came even closer, he knew that he knew him well, and at less than a hundred feet away, he knew that the man was Alex. Walking faster, then galloping into a run, Will ran to his son.

Alex had stopped walking when Will finally got to him, had turned to stare at the water. He glanced at Will, then back to the water. If Alex recognized him, he didn't say.

"Alex," said Will, "how are you?"

"I'm fine."

"Are you waiting for something?"

Alex pointed at a flag stuck into the sand up the beach. It was a red pennant stuck onto a wooden dowel rod. "Waiting for a ride."

"To where?"

"The other side," said Alex, smiling. "I've got just enough money." Will's son held his hand out, palm open, and Will could see three silver dollars, utterly unlike any silver dollars he'd ever seen. Richard Nixon had replaced Kennedy, and the minting of the money had been done poorly. They looked cheaply made. "Where are you headed, mister?" Alex asked him.

"I don't know. I just woke up here. Do you recognize me?"

"No."

"We know each other, though. How else would I have known your name?"

Alex shrugged and put the change back in his pocket. "I don't know. I just figured you knew mine, but I didn't know yours. It happens."

"I suppose."

"Do you have money for the ferryman?"

"No," said Will, checking the pockets on his shorts. "I don't have anything."

"He's not going to let you on the boat. Look, you can see him coming now."

Alex was right. Will could see a boat coming. For some reason, the sight of it made him feel sick. Watching the boat come closer, Will could see that it was all black, a bigger boat, but not a yacht like some folks kept in the lakes. He could see a dog on the prow of the boat, an ugly black thing, and he could hear its barking carried by the wind. Twin smells—sulfur and shit—were coming from the lake, and Will could see steam rising from the water. Looking at the bridge, Will would have sworn that it was broken, shattered into the water. He blinked, and it was normal, yet warped somehow. The Mac, but not.

Alex peeled off his shirt and said, "Time for me to go, mister."

Will watched him walk into the water, never flinching at the heat, just wading into it until it was deep enough for him to swim, and then Alex was slowly swimming to the boat, which was now less than fifty feet from shore.

The dog was much more clearly visible now. It was barking and roaring aboard the slowly rocking boat, and then Will could see Alex aboard the black vessel. There was a man there, and Will wanted to shout to Alex, to tell him to get back in the water, to swim back, that there would be another boat, a better one. Instead, Will watched Alex fish in his pocket and drop the coins into the man's gloved hand. The man closed his fist.

**W**hen Will woke, he saw Alison's face. There was a machine making a screaming, beeping noise, and he felt sure that he was in Lou's office, the last seconds of his life playing out as he died. It wasn't quite his life flashing before his eyes, but it could have been a lot worse. He found himself trying to speak, trying to move his arms and legs, but everything was frozen, as though he were glued to the floor with some insanely strong industrial adhesive.

Suddenly, Alison was gone, her face replaced by the face of someone he didn't know. The beeping grew louder, and an incredible force smashed into his chest.

She was there the second time he woke, holding his hand. She was talking to someone, facing away from him. He tried to squeeze back, but he couldn't, he had no strength. There were still machines beeping, but none of them were shrieking. He smiled, or at least he felt like he did, and gave her hand another squeeze. Her head snapped toward him, her face more beautiful in that moment than it had ever been, her eyes like fireworks. She said something, her voice coming from underwater, and then she was gone, yelling something.

Alison was back moments later, grabbing his arm, trying to ask him something, a repetitive question, repeated like a cadence, that slowly unearthed itself. When he could finally hear her, he felt like an archaeologist must as he excavates a giant femur from some long-dead lizard.

"Will? Can you hear me?"

"Yes," said Will, his voice slow and syrupy, foreign to him, as if he'd been drugged. "Yes, I can hear you. Where am I?"

"At the hospital," she said, then clarified, "at Spectrum. You were shot twice. You almost died." Her eyes were welling with tears, and they were sparkling in the hospital light. "You almost died, do you understand?"

"Yes. But I'm going to be OK?"

"I don't know. No one knows. They didn't expect you to be awake yet. I can't believe I almost lost you."

"Are Isaac and Jason OK?"

"Yes, they're fine. Well, better than you, at any rate. I honestly can't believe you're OK."

Someone that Will couldn't see was talking to Alison. He could hear little bits of words, but nothing that really came through or made much sense.

Alison turned back to him again, smiling warmly. "Will, they want you to sleep a little longer, OK?"

"No," said Will, "it's not OK. I'm fine."

He would have kept going, but then a numbness, starting in his left hand, was washing over his body, and she was gone, the hospital was gone, and finally, the bed was gone underneath him. He was floating in a white world, and then everything else was gone too, even the white.

* * *

Will woke again. This time he was sitting up in a raised bed. He was still in the hospital, still hooked to beeping machines, though he was quite sure now that there were fewer of them, or at least these were quieter.

Alison wasn't in the room, but there was a young black woman sitting across the room at a table next to an older white man. The two, noticing him stir, stood and crossed the room to him.

"Mr. Daniels, I'm Dr. Monroe," said the black woman, then gestured to the older man, "and this is Dr. Halleck. We have both been involved in your care up to this point, Mr. Daniels, along with a great many other people."

"Thank you. I appreciate it very much."

The two doctors smiled, and the older one spoke.

"You are out of the woods, Mr. Daniels, though not by much. You were shot twice, once through your right hip and then again through your collarbone. You are very, very lucky to be alive. The bullet in your hip really should have severed your femoral artery, and if that had happened, you would be dead. You are going to be in a wheelchair for a little while, and walking is going to be rough, possibly for the rest of your life. Take that as a good thing. You are likely to walk again, assuming you do your part in physical therapy, but it is possible that you will have mobility issues. I'm sure that's hard to hear, but you'll adjust. Just remember that you ought to be dead, and uncomfortable days will still seem bearable."

"As happy as we are to see you, and to give you some news on your current condition," said Dr. Monroe, "we are also here to make sure that you're physically and mentally ready to talk to the police. There is a detective here that has been very eager to speak with you."

"Van Endel?"

"Yes," both doctors said, answering at the same time, but with only Dr. Monroe continuing to speak. "Detective Van Endel has been waiting for a little more than a week. If you're not ready yet, I can tell him to bug off, but you're going to need to talk to him eventually. He has the look of a man very used to getting what he wants."

"If I talk to him, can I see my wife afterwards?"

"You can see her either way, Mr. Daniels," said Dr. Halleck, frowning. "Neither Dr. Monroe or myself are offering you a carrot on a stick, nor do we even feel pressed to do so at this point.

If you want to talk to the detective and then your wife, that's fine. If you prefer your wife first, or even just her, that's fine as well."

"I can talk to Van Endel. Will you send him in with some water? I'm really thirsty."

"Of course," said Dr. Monroe, but the look on her face had changed. "Mr. Daniels, as far as we know, you have not been charged with a crime. If you want the detective to leave, press the call button by your right hand, and one of us will be in shortly."

Will watched them leave, and a few minutes later, Van Endel entered the room. The detective was carrying a Styrofoam cup with a bendy straw sticking out of the top of it, along with another cup that Will guessed to be coffee. Van Endel set the water down on a table next to Will's hospital bed, then picked up one of the chairs the doctors had been using and moved it closer to the bed.

"How are you, Will?"

"I've been better."

"I bet."

"What happened? The last thing I remember was Lou pointing a gun in my face."

"Well, Mr. Schultz was in the act of executing you when three of our SWAT officers breached the room. They used flashbangs, a type of grenade that makes a white flash instead of an explosion. It can be very debilitating, at least temporarily. The first of those exploded at almost the exact moment that you were shot, causing Mr. Schultz to move the barrel and shoot you in the chest, instead of the head. The first member of the team saw Mr. Schultz trying to aim at you again, and killed him. You were very lucky."

"So Lou's dead."

"Yes."

"Aren't you supposed to be asking me the questions? I sort of feel like we're going in reverse."

"I'm making an appearance, Mr. Daniels, nothing more. Officially, the matter is settled. You were visiting your attorney when he turned on you. He was later found to have high levels of painkillers, cocaine, and alcohol in his system."

"Was the other guy dead?"

"Yes, Carlos Santiago is dead. He was a very, very dangerous man, Will. You're lucky to have spent any time near him and survived at all. He liked machetes a great deal when he was just a young man. The DEA has been trying to get a handle on Carlos for a long time; he was one of the biggest stateside names in MS-Thirteen."

"What about the pictures?"

"What pictures?"

"You know what pictures. The ones of the mayor." Will could hear the frustration coming out in his voice, and he took a drink of water. "The pictures on Lou's desk, of Mayor Huntington and a young girl, they were awful."

"Will, I'm going to say this exactly one time, all right? If there were some pictures of the mayor doing something so utterly awful that it pains me to even think about it, they were gone by the time my men got there. If such pictures had existed, or if someone were to have made copies or otherwise attempt to prove their existence, I am quite sure they could be easily proven to be manipulated photography. However, if such pictures existed and they were given to someone like me, I would use them to force the mayor's hand in a few issues you're unaware of and, once those matters are dealt with, see that he retires. These are things I can *barely* do, Will. You would be killed if you tried.

"On a side note, there were DNA samples found for the three of you—Jason, Isaac, and you, I mean—at the house of one Christopher 'Mumbo' Jefferson. Mumbo was found strangled to death; it looked like he was tortured as well."

"He was at the bank with Alex."

"Will, I know why you did exactly what you did. There's a part of me, a non-cop part, that even sort of admires it. The rest of me, though…well, the rest thinks you're a fucking idiot who was cheating death left and right.

"Forget about the pictures. They're long gone, and you're still here. You want to take some time, recover. Get back to work. There's nothing you can do about the rest, and if you try, your luck is going to run out fast."

"What was Lou doing?"

"He was doing the only thing that men like him know how to do—he was trying to make a deal while he was treading water. A blackmail plan seems the most likely, so let that be what helps you sleep at night. Even if Mr. Schultz had used the pictures or sold them like he wanted to the highest bidder, they were never going to get released. They were taken to try and destroy a man, and there was never going to be any courtroom justice for the victim, no matter what you did, or do in the future. I, on the other hand, can see them brought to some use, albeit still under the radar of an ordinary citizen. Is that clear enough?"

"I'm just wondering what pictures you were talking about."

Van Endel smiled thinly, finished his coffee or whatever it was in the cup, and threw it in the garbage.

"Good luck."

"Thanks."

**W**riting came back. It was hard at times, but Will fought the headaches that would come raging out of nowhere with time away from the keyboard. Time with Alison. Writing before had been an escape, a rope thrown to a drowning man; now it was just something that he did, something he was. Alison gave him the space that he needed but somehow was always there when that same space was unnecessary. It was as though she had a window into his mind.

The first book after everything was over, and two weeks after physical therapy had begun, was about recovery. It didn't start that way, and it didn't end that way, but that's what it was all the same. Will took the sweat of the therapy sessions and used that as a catalyst to give his character legs, and then in a cruel moment of keyboard indulgence, Will took the legs away, and his character came to life.

Equally important to the development of his character was heart. That critical organ started beating the day Will saw on the news that Mayor Huntington was stepping down. Whatever Van Endel had needed to do, he'd gotten done. Will went back to his writing after watching the report and could feel the blood surging through his fingertips into his protagonist.

He talked to Jack often as he wrote, giving his friend, so many miles away, short updates on his writing, his beaten body, and his mental state. All were getting better. When the manuscript, with the working title of *Broken Bastard*, was finished, Will sent it off to Terri, not with the fear of rejection that had always plagued him, but with a bizarre confidence. His publisher loved it, and the game of updates, contracts, and conference calls began again.

Life was as normal as it was going to get, and that was just fine with Will and Alison.

**T**hey stood as a group of five. Will, Alison, Isaac and his wife, Daisy, and Jason. In Will's hands was a container holding Alex's ashes, and he could see the Mackinac Bridge if he looked to his right.

Will walked alone into the water and began to sprinkle the ashes into the lake, watching as the waves slowly took his son into the water. Down the beach, Will could see a man staring at them—staring, it seemed, at him. When Will had emptied the container of his son's ashes, he ignored the stranger, dressed so much like Alex had been in the dream, and walked to Alison. He took his wife in his arms and embraced her, but when he looked back, the man was gone, and the ashes were lost to the waves.

# ACKNOWLEDGMENTS

**O**n October 13th, 2011, Walker Police Officer Trevor Slot received a phone call from his wife, Kim. The cancer was back, and it was in her spine. "Don't worry," he said. "It'll be OK." She could hear the stress in his voice; something else was wrong. "Hon, I've got to go." Those were the last words they spoke, as Officer Slot was killed just moments later by two fleeing bank robbers as he attempted to lay down spike sticks in an effort to disable their car. The robbers, armed and shooting at police, were killed minutes later.

I never met Trevor Slot, though he lived just a couple of streets from me, and our daughters attend the same elementary school. We were close enough that I heard the cancer story before the media did, hushed whispers between mothers of other small children, talking about how sad it all was, how tragic. Yet, as sad as it all was, it was something else too. It was heroic.

Officer Slot gave his life to maintain public order. Not as a sacrificial lamb, but as a genuine badass, likely in the sort of way that the people who knew him outside of work, friends from church perhaps, never would have seen. Weeks later, I saw his wife and kids as my friend Scott and I took our daughters trick-or-treating along the usual route. Officer Slot's family had nothing but smiles and hellos for everyone. It would have been easy to shut off the lights and not participate. Apparently, that wouldn't have been good enough.

Officer Slot was the purest definition of a rough man. He knew every day when he put on his uniform what the risks were, and that for him, they were worth bearing. He is, quite literally, the kind of man that allowed us on that fateful day to live our lives safely, without even being aware that violence was afoot. Much thanks to all of you in law enforcement and the armed services who do the same.

At the time of this writing, it is my understanding that Mrs. Slot's cancer is inactive. I wish her all the best in her battle with this terrible illness and look forward to seeing her for many Halloweens to come.

* * *

Endless thanks to my endlessly supportive family, who have helped this writer endure stress beyond measure. The most-affected victims being, of course, my wife and daughter, who are far more wonderful and loving than anyone I deserve to have in my life, but yet continue to stick around and support me, even through the frustrations of writing. A simple thanks would never be enough, but it's all I've got. I love you both so much.

My parents, equally as supportive, are also deserving of a round of applause and perhaps a few high fives. Through their tireless efforts to help, listen to, and bolster this writer's confidence, I manage to maintain the ability to sit alone before a keyboard and make imaginary friends absolutely miserable. Again, a simple thank-you would never be enough.

A thanks as well to my dear friend—and editor—Terry, of Amazon, who made the third time a charm for me, and of course, offered the kind of wisdom to help make this book everything that it could be. Additional kudos to my partner in the lab, David. Three books down, and this one edited faster than the rest, I truly feel like we're forming some sort of superheroesque duo, and that we could likely edit a book in the most dire of circumstances, and at lightning speed.

Thanks to my good friend Jacque for her efforts in supporting her "kids," her childlike author stable of man-creatures and woman-beasts, which she does a wonderful job wrangling, and to whom I offer a simple quote, from a simple man: "A woman is a lot like a refrigerator. Six feet tall, 300 pounds…it makes ice."

Thanks to another good friend, Ms. Sarah Burningham of Little Bird Publicity, who has done so much for my career that it seems sort of impossible, and has also given me a shoulder to whine into on more than one occasion. As with everyone else on this list, I can't say thank-you enough, and I truly hope we work together again. Not only for selfish reasons—you are the best—but also because you're a sheer joy to talk to and work with. Also, by the time this book is released, I can say, "Congrats!"

To everyone at Amazon and Brilliance Audio, kudos for your efforts on my behalf, and though there are far too many of you to name, I will try. Thanks to smooth-talking Luke Daniels, Sarah T., Rory, Alex, Katie of 47 North, Patrick of 47 North, Megan, editor Jessica, editor Ashley, all the folks at Thomas and Mercer, and everyone I forgot, thank you all so much.

To my first readers, Dad, Greg, and Jacque, thanks, as always, for helping with early feedback and confidence restoration.

One last thing: thank you.

# ABOUT THE AUTHOR

The author of *A Good and Useful Hurt*, *Nickel Plated*, and *From Ashes Rise*, Aric Davis brings a unique flavor to his writing thanks to his sixteen-year career as a body piercer and punk-rock aficionado. Alongside reading and writing, he takes special delight in roller coasters, hockey, chilly weather, and honest friends. He lives in Grand Rapids, Michigan, with his wife and daughter.